BEYOND THESE WINTERS

BEYOND THESE WINTERS

Liese Jeyd Hartman

Cress Branch Books

For Emma and Delilah

Ruins

In that last evening before she lost everything, the fox pondered the skyscrapers that appeared to push out of the water, their broken windows flashing in the sun's retreat. The sleek yacht glided past nonchalantly, its electric motor humming. Fen peered over the rail, then settled back into the deck chair where she prepared for the interminable evening.

Her soft fur shifted hues to match her emotions: blue, mauve, and then blue again. Her radiant brush of a tail tucked around her snout and she rested for the moment, satiated with what she had seen. Scents of seagulls and salty air clouded her thoughts. She pressed them all away. Instead, she allowed herself to passively listen to the conversation around her, though no one was saying anything she cared to hear.

On the deck, four expensively dressed passengers reclined in plush chairs, sipping drinks as they took in the remnants of another drowned city along the coastline. They were on holiday, surveying the Atlantic coast from a safe distance. Fen despised them, and they ignored her, seeming to know she would bite them if they tried to touch her shimmering form.

"I heard this city used to be quite the destination," said Beale lazily, glancing left. His hair was combed upward in a stylish wave, and a diamond pin flashed boldly on his lapel.

"Did it?" asked Marion, stifling a yawn. "It's not much to look at now." Marion and Menora wore vintage cocktail dresses and both vied for Beale's attention. Fen knew the twins had tried to woo Canto once, but he'd been repulsed by their haughtiness.

"It hardly matters, does it?" said Menora, her eyes half-lidded with boredom. "Just a relic, like everything else we've seen. But there's a certain melancholy beauty."

The others murmured agreement. The fox's fur transitioned to a mournful gray as she thought again of the buildings passing by. It was late afternoon, and she dreaded another evening on deck. Canto was sick. That meant deck time for her, which was something worse than isolation. Everyone always tried to outdo one another. Who had the highest hair? Whose jewelry had the best story? Where were the best drinks? Fen grimaced and buried her face more deeply into her tail.

"I do wish we'd encounter some other boats, though," Menora complained to no one in particular. "It's frightfully dull."

Fen lifted her head and then rested her chin on her paws. Dull? Wasn't the point of travel to learn the story of a place? To see the marks of history? To marvel in nature's shaping power? Behind Fen's eyes, advanced processes whirred in tandem with her organic brain, evaluating and analyzing. She had been designed to understand and empathize with humans, and also to remember. As she tapped into the onboard computer, Fen immersed herself in the story of the last century.

She listened once more as the virtual guide described how climate change had ravaged coastlines and forced mass migrations inland toward more temperate zones nearer the poles. Entire regions had become uninhabitable wastelands. Sea levels had risen dramatically, weather had grown savage and unpredictable. She had heard it all before, when Canto was planning for the trip.

With a small sigh, Fen wished Canto would return for her. As she drowsily closed her eyes, the computer she linked to offered a pleasant guided tour. This voice was more upbeat than the one she had listened to the day before. "We are currently paralleling the submerged remnants of Miami Beach, once a popular oceanside resort."

"Oh Beale darling, you simply must see the new terraformed gardens at my summer estate," trilled Marion ecstatically. "I'll have my social secretary send you an invite." Her hand extended and grasped the hem of his sleeve.

The drone of voices and the constant thrum of waves soon had Fen drifting into vivid dreams where past and present collided. A panorama of the bustling seaside flickered through her mind. Laughing families crowded the beach, gulls wheeled in the golden light. The relentless ocean devoured the sand, decade by decade. Ghostly towers flanked empty transient camps, a field of tattered and faded tents.

"As you can see," continued the cheerful voice, "The geography along this coastline experienced significant erosion starting in the late 21st century."

"Of course!" Beale exclaimed. "We'll have to flit over to Misi's newest club afterward. I heard the artificials look so realistic you can barely tell." Misi gazed smugly at the twins, and fingered her emerald pendant conspicuously. Beale had given it to her this morning, and she wanted the others to see.

Fen twitched her tail occasionally while the guide continued its coastal history narration: "Miami Beach was once a vibrant tourist destination known for its Art Deco architecture, sandy beaches and glittering nightlife. As ocean levels rose, it became ground zero for the climate change crisis in the late 2000s and the insurance crash—"

"This vessel is dreadfully small! My yacht is four times this size." From the upper lounge, Marion's shrill voice wafted down.

"Mine has a full botanical garden in the glass atrium," Menora said. "Beale darling, didn't you just upgrade after that horrifying incident?" She glanced over at the sleeping Fen, as if the fox were to blame for every remote unit designed to incorporate technology with organics. Birds were especially useful, though conspicuous if they didn't employ chroma tech. Her family's wealth derived from genetic cloaking in creatures like Fen and armor for military equipment.

The ability to camouflage one's fur or render a surface nearly invisible had been one of the great advancements of the century. Why Canto needed this quality in a pet was beyond her. It didn't even know how to hide itself, Menora thought, but sat here changing colors for no reason. Menora scowled at Fen, who heard the thoughts that Menora threw at her like stones. The inane prattle faded away as Fen sank deeper into dreams.

"By 2115, the eastern coast of Florida was declared uninhabitable," intoned the guide. "Millions fled the relentless advancing seas and extreme weather to resettle farther inland."

Fen saw panicked families cramming the highways in an endless exodus. Bedraggled climate refugees struggled through storm-torn landscapes. Angry waves engulfed the glittering shore. Gradually the lights went out, one by one. The city became dark with decay.

The fox awoke with a sudden shudder as Marion's cackling laughter echoed across the deck.

But like the waves, the tour guide's soothing voice soon overwhelmed everything else. "By the year 2130, humanity had settled into a new normal after the traumas of the climate crisis era."

Fen's dozing mind painted vivid scenes to match the narration. How the weary refugees moved inland and adopted sustainable lifestyles. How merchant sailors risked the Arctic sea lanes, how others collected steel along the inland rails. Canto had once called it the economy of adaptation. He saw it as fruitful and positive. They were supposed to be gathering information for his company's expansion south, but instead, everyone stayed close to the comfort of the yacht.

Fen heard the rich sightseers lounging on deck, oblivious and indifferent as their luxurious yacht passed over the very lands where these hardships had played out just a generation before. Fen attuned her auditory sensors to the banal chatter floating down from above.

"These flooded ruins are just terribly depressing," came Marion's nasal complaint. "Honestly, it's all a bit much—" She was swaying a bit and laughed when the yacht surged forward with unexpected speed. Everyone giggled. Perhaps someone had fallen against the controls. In the minds of the affluent passengers, the crew was an inconvenient necessity, and incompetent at that.

Fen's soft fur gradually shifted again, now slate blue. She

longed for Canto, wishing he was there to explain things. Why the past mattered. How all these things were connected.

Much of the rainforest was gone, though new forests had been planted on other continents. The gold had been mined from every dead-eyed pit long ago. The central deserts of North America and Europe transformed the way people would travel and interact. People still living on the Atlantic coast accepted their lives because, at least, they *were* alive, and had remained in place after most people had chosen to go elsewhere.

Elsewhere meant there was an alternative. For many, it was simply to leave ahead of some doom to come. Whether they found something better, no one could say. It was still too early to tell where these stories would go, and who would people them.

As the waves lapped rhythmically, the fox rested her head. The soundtracks overlapped and clashed. Fen surrendered to restless visions far from the opulent, aimless world around her.

The Courier

To Rilke, the first days after a hurricane were signs of new hell to come. The wind and waves dislodged residents and scrambled whatever order had begun to form. New eyes watched him from broken windows that were empty before. The roads and alleys were always changed. But by the third day, the waters had receded and the trash had already been picked over by scavengers that walked on two legs and also four.

Here and there, Rilke would encounter a path still covered in water and rerouted without stopping. Then he'd quicken his pace and take the turns he knew would get him back home. It was never simple, and the storms always took more than they gave back. But Rilke was accustomed to the streets and the way some roads dipped down into the water permanently and disappeared into preceding decades.

Briefly, he stopped to decipher a shredded notice on a papered wall. He glanced over his shoulder, then back to the tattered signs. Rilke didn't often notice the graffiti or flyers, even the little shrines his mother had warned him about in his youth. He did notice the breeze when it finally picked up again. It bore the heaviness of sea air with the taint of rot, and the creatures who were still feasting.

Rilke didn't dwell on the past of the world, before the mass migrations toward the more temperate North. This was because history had always been invisible to him. He had lived his childhood in the ruined stadium downtown, closest to the water. No one he personally knew had ever seen the things he read about or heard described at school. This uncertainty made a young person want to be sent away, not because his parents were cruel or because life was difficult, but because there was nothing worth knowing in a world no one believed in anymore.

But then he found a book of Rainer Maria Rilke's poems, and with it, a new name.

He enjoyed reading aloud, sounding out the words he did not know and finding a resonant hum in his chest. For him, reciting Rilke to himself in the loneliness of his tiny room was the closest thing to a spiritual undertaking he could know.

Like that poet who had lived so long ago, Rilke was a quiet and gentle person. His brown eyes observed everything, and he said little. What he did say was usually too soft to be heard. The exception would be the time he spent alone reading his book of poems to himself, sounding out the syllables, sometimes trying the German as well with indistinct and timid emphasis. The English was easier, though not the only language he had heard in the stadium growing up. But English was what he had learned to read in the schools, and he had taken to it quickly. Printed words appeared to him in a way he understood. The revelatory and profound silences between words were where he had always found himself. He craved the imagery of a place and time different from the one he already knew.

Rilke had begun his recitals shortly after finding the book in a beaten box wedged behind a screen door. It was an abandoned house he'd tried delivering to, before realizing he had the wrong address. The box had caught his eye because it seemed out of place. Why would it be left there? And how had no one seen it until he came along? He had looked around him to see if it were a trick, perhaps another way to catch him and hold him still, like a trap of attention. But no one was around and he saw no hiding places where someone could be in the shadows, watching.

In a time when many people would find empty houses and dwell in them, he worked for credits which housed him. His key allowed access to his home where he lived alone. Many years before, when he had lived in the stadium with his ma and Afi, there had always been a need to find food or to grow it. Many people had plots in the broken green spaces where they grew squash or corn. His mother grew tomatoes, onions, and garlic. His uncle knew how to hunt gators which existed in such numbers that there were always more to be found.

Before the kid had found the book of Rilke's poetry, the only stories he knew were the ones his ma or uncle told. There was the one about an old man who slept under the same lamp post every night, waiting for his brother to pick him up, though no one ever did. During a freak snowstorm in early summer he had frozen there, standing up. So the people remembered him and left oddly-shaped stones or walking sticks against the wall nearest the lamp. Rilke's ma said this was to remind everyone that staying in one place didn't reward them. Instead, it brought the stillness which kills, when people can't change and won't move forward.

Rilke's ma told stories like these that always meant more than the details in them. But he was fascinated by the images in his mind of stones, stacked one upon another. The line of walking sticks leaning or having fallen. The frozen beard of the old man and the icicle of snot they said was inches long. Rilke had never seen snow, so this story was especially memorable.

"Child, this is not the way to live, standing on corners waiting," his ma would say with a fierce, pointing finger thrust close to his face. "You have to move, *move*, MOVE, I say!"

Her large body was always pushing out from some piece of clothing that was too small for her. She moved with the confidence of a woman who knew what she needed for survival and used all of it. He admired her, but didn't know if he loved her. Not, and certainly never, in the way the poet Rilke had loved the world he saw and described in his poems.

When Rilke remembered his ma, he also remembered uncles. They might have been brothers or fathers or cousins, but a family could take many forms. Rilke's ma and Uncle Afi had come from further west. They had decided to be brother and sister to one another, and this is how Rilke remembered them. He never felt like the name they had given him was his. He sometimes told himself late at night that he would name himself when he heard the name that belonged to his soul. For him, *Rilke* had been that name.

It was most certainly a world where people became sick with memory or they forgot or became forgotten. But these were the people Rilke had known at the stadium, and nowhere else. The rainforest his ma had remembered from her grandmother's stories, and her great-grandmother's stories, was part of a world that had ceased being deep forest and was now a drying grassland. Everything good had been mined out of it.

Uncle Afi taught him how to hunt gator. When Rilke was with Afi, he thought of his ma in a more friendly way. He simultaneously hated and loved her. The hate was really some kind of fear, but of what he didn't have a name for. The love was some kind of feeling that he knew he was supposed to have but could not recognize.

Rilke leaned more heavily toward nights on the boat with his uncle when he remembered life in the stadium. That time spent on the boat drove his desire to explore the world. In himself too, he also had a preference to not worry about food ever again. He did not want to sit on a bloodstained boat with his uncle at twilight, hunting gator.

"This," lectured his uncle during those lessons, "is a fifty-pound-test line." Rilke noticed its heaviness and nodded approvingly. It had been like this every time, but in all cases, he had been excited and also stricken with terror. Perhaps he would have to haul the gator in himself this time and he wouldn't be ready. But then he was reassured that his uncle was there and he could count on Afi if there was a problem.

"Now," said his uncle, staring steadily at him, "is when we use the gig." He always held everything patiently for Rilke to study.

"We mount it . . . so."

Afi always fitted the archery tackle and drew it on a crossbow he'd crafted for this purpose. Whenever they snagged one, Afi would run a snare around the gator's snout with a long pole. Nearby was the bangstick, which was applied to the skull of the gator before bringing it into the boat. Afi always wrapped their jaws carefully because they sometimes appeared dead, but weren't. That's when Afi would raise his scarred and misshapen hand, then speak of Rilke's mother.

"She made herself a bed in my soul, your ma." He looked down, his hat shielding his eyes, and stared at his hand. "She found me in the bayou. She saved my life."

And that was how Rilke best remembered his Uncle Afi, and why decades later certain lines from the poet would always stand out to him: She "made herself a bed in my ear," which was the same but not really. The poet had written in his own language, *in meinum Ohr*, and *ohr* sounded to him like "hour" but also like "oar," which is what Rilke stared at whenever his uncle talked of his life debt to Rilke's ma. It was clear they were not brother and sister but people accepted the idea, because his ma would never have married Afi and his uncle was never at home with his ma like a father was supposed to be. But still they were a part of his life like the ocean was, and like the broken streets of the city gradually became.

Rilke knew even then he wanted free of their stories and had to leave. He didn't want to leave Afi alone and yet was driven to because his mother had always told him to "Move, move, move!" She overwhelmed him with hard and practical instruction, every day, without Afi's patience. Sometimes she would bop his head with her calloused hand and mumble something incomprehensible. Then he would find the old car seat that had always been in the stadium and rock until he felt better or until someone sat down beside him and that would sometimes help too.

He often thought of that junked car seat when the state officials would come to his classroom and ask the students questions about their lives and what they would do in this or that hypothetical situation. Everything was *this or that* in those days, during the long century after the longest anyone had ever known. It was the twenty-second, and here he had been, a twelve-year-old Rilke hunting gator with his uncle. Something in him said "Move!" and it was deeper and more profound than even his ma could be when she was angry, so he accepted those words as the prophetic message of his life.

Expansive Sky

Rilke smelled the beach on the warm October wind and followed the poles that carried invisible transmissions across the city. He ignored the lines, just as he did the junk piles and grubby-faced children or the broken porches of his deliveries. He had given up expecting pleasantries after his first few days as a courier. Rilke's curly hair sprung in coils around his face like a halo, and this sometimes made him appear younger than his nineteen years. His identity and his job intersected, and there was only "You! I have a delivery," or more simply, "Kid!" Sometimes, he ran away without making eye contact. Conversation was frequently a lure and he couldn't afford to be kind.

Rilke preferred anonymity. The city itself had become anonymous in that long century after its decline. If he could make it to work and home without encountering anyone, it was a good day. His deliveries were the only part that included people, and on the side of town considered much safer. He was lucky to have the route coveted among Kasim's couriers. Kasim was good to him, and referred to Rilke as "brother." Everyone was *brother* or *sister* to Kasim, and they came to his bakery for his kindness as much as the bread and halal meats he sold for fair prices.

Rilke wrapped one arm around his depleted duffel and glanced around the corner. No one today, thankfully. Sometimes he'd seen a group of kids on this street, kicking a ball around. Like conversation, a game could also carry risk. A year before, he'd stopped to play, and set his bag down, full of leftover rolls that were his dinner. He'd not make the same mistake again. The slender youth jogged across the debris-littered street into the shade of a tree as its bulging roots crawled out from a cracked cement planter. Here he readied his key before looking both ways and ducking toward his door. He usually came a different way home every few days. So far, it had kept him safe.

Rilke lived alone in the back half of a decades-old bungalow. His part of the house was a creaky-floored room with a tub so small his knees pressed up uncomfortably. He washed quickly, weekly, and habitually in tepid water. He cleaned his mouth in the main room's sink, and captured the drinking water he would need for that day. Lately it had been occurring to him that his life had become work, and work was just to have a room to sleep in and food to fullness. If there was more to life, he wasn't sure what that could be.

The next day Rilke walked through the city, dodging alleys that had closed themselves off with makeshift gates. Backyards were unlikely to be sanctuary for just one person, and Rilke knew to avoid them. But if he was going to find anything to salvage from the storm, today was his best chance. He didn't have to work, so he'd spent the morning reading and thinking about where to scavenge. He took up his delivery duffel and exited the house after stealing a cautious glimpse through the peep hole.

Each day was like any other, but not this one. Poetic lines formed in his mind as syllables from his readings. These syllables lodged in words like "star" and "radiance" and the idea of it being dead for thousands of years even though he could still feel its light on his skin. This thought was the beginning of something new, he was sure of it. Why were these lines of the poet coming to him now?

For Rilke, words could emerge without a book in his hands or his seeing them, but they were no less real. They were not his words, but he felt them. They described something like resignation, but also had the flavor of despair. Perhaps this is how his uncle had felt when he had almost lost his hand. Or, when Rilke himself had watched while a stranger coughed blood, just before falling over. His ma's haste had been terrifying when they pulled the collapsed stranger into their tent.

"Hurry. Grab what's good," she had said, and they rifled through the man's pockets in a way that Rilke had felt bad about though he didn't know why. It was just his time to go, his ma said later.

The feelings that he could not describe without these other feelings gave him the vocabulary of his days.

But this day spoke more loudly than all the others.

He didn't experience nostalgia or hopefulness that people did when they had once had everything then lost it. He was instead moving from a kind of deprivation toward something he could not yet see. Rilke knew that something was different, but he did not yet know how or why. More strange words arrived unbidden.

"I would like to step out from my heart under the

expansive sky."

There, again. It was as if he was being heard by something larger than himself when he said the words into the air, though they were not his words, but those of a dead German poet from four centuries before.

"Expansive sky!" he shouted, and marveled at the sound of his voice so loud, reverberating against empty parking garages and deserted buildings. When he thought the words, they shouted inside his mind, and when he shouted them into the air, for anyone on that street to hear, everything within him became silent. The contradiction puzzled him, but he kept walking. He quickened his step, just in case the shout had invited some threat into the streets. His pace became a slight bounce verging on a jog.

He turned onto the edge of the street that in another time had been lined with parked cars, but was made much narrower by the scrap that choked the sidewalks. Most of the heaps were decades old, formed from the leavings of families who chose to evacuate the city. He kept to the path through the high grasses lining what had once been a walkway.

"One must be able to think back on paths in unknown regions, on unexpected encounters" he muttered, savoring the idea of thinking back, and then also, discovery.

He stopped to catch his breath and wondered whether his nightly readings made him more vulnerable to stray thoughts. Rilke wondered what kind of world the poet had lived in, to have spent so much time describing what felt familiar to him but also strange and otherworldly. To have written so much about loneliness and sorrow, but to have been filled with voices and joy.

When the next line came, he did not hold back, but spoke the words aloud to himself, savoring their delicious accuracy. "Your way through the people you do not understand becomes ever more solitary."

To Rilke, most people were difficult to understand. "Even more so perhaps in vain, to maintain direction, maintain direction towards the future, towards that which is lost." He paused, staring at a wall beginning to crumble from the utmost corner and the scrubby pines clinging to the embankment. Could lost futures be retrieved?

Chilling lines from Rilke's poems and letters sometimes clogged the kid's thoughts like knots of startled birds' wings. The idea of death being everywhere, even in nails jutting from old boards. That a nail could celebrate and dream of death, of causing harm. Yet he did remember the times, years ago, when he played among the rafters of the stadium when a cut would make him feel singled out. Pain always made him feel more alone than when he was well.

Thoughts like these made him glance over his shoulder and shiver. He looked for a different way to get to the beach than his usual path. This he did without questioning. His city had taught him about gut instinct, and how one should always listen to internal messages of danger that came without warning. His alternate path took him behind a wall, through a corridor usually avoided but now a better way.

Immediately he was reassured when the corridor opened to the side of a cliff, or what had once been the topside of an overpass. This was before the original highway had become a swampy estuary, welcoming the sea into the city's low places. He looked across to other streets now underwater and the crooked skeletal structures that had long since been salvaged for steel, and whatever else had been valuable then.

That was when he heard the whimper tucked into the broken shrubs ahead of him. The pause he took was a long one.

He listened to the tension welling up inside his intestines, but not from alarm. What he felt instead was more like what he felt the day he'd found his book of poetry tucked inside the door of the abandoned house. Curious, he inched forward. He slowly inclined his head as he knelt and met the gaze of an animal unlike anything he had ever seen.

Rilke froze in place and once again queried his instinct. He spoke a word aloud, softly to the creature that stared directly into his eyes, as he saw himself reflected in hers. "Help?"

"Help," echoed the amber eyes. He did not have to ask whether the word had come from her.

"Please," she said, through a language that Rilke had never heard before, but found exhilarating. He had only seen an animal like her in pictures, but she was considerably more exotic.

Her face was rimmed with a feathery softness that reflected light in every direction. Her ears stood out from her head in great triangles, tufted with shimmery threads of multiple colors. Her body was lithe, the blast of fur extending from her neck but becoming less full along her silvery torso and legs. Her feet ended in toes with berry-brown pads and little retractable claws a centimeter long. Her tail bushed out into a massive oval with downy tendrils.

While studying her, the word *fox* came to Rilke's mind from a book at school. Even so, she was not like the image in his second grade letter book. She was no quick, brown fox but an iridescent one, filled with a spectrum of color and wondrous, even gentle in her expression. There was a pain there too, one Rilke understood even though he had not seen a being like her before.

"Carry," the fox said. He looked down at his rough coveralls and tried to clean his palms in a gesture he had never tried before. In his world, everything was soiled and nothing was ever clean. But he tried to prepare his hands for the radiant fur that appeared luminous and pure amid the flood-dirt of the bank.

"Use sack."

Of course, he thought. If he found her strange and magical, how would she appear to anyone else? He needed to conceal her glimmering form.

Rilke untied the sack from his belt and positioned it so that she could wriggle inside, with minimal help. She was on a small shelf of muddy rock, so her angle assisted with her movement, though he could sense how weak she was.

"Must rest now," came to him in a soft rush. He studied his hand which carried a small amount of pearlescent dust.

The fox seemed to know that Rilke would not hurt her and that staying where he had found her was risky. Having never been lost before, she did not know what else to do. Nowhere in her banks of memory had she ever known the absence of human protection. She had always lived in controlled environments where her every whim was fulfilled. Some would see her as an expensive pet, and despite the many foolish transactions human beings made with each other, she had surely never been such a transaction herself, she thought.

Lost.

She had no sense of what the word could mean, just as she did not know words like *alone, frightened,* or *hungry.* More precisely, she had not known the words until a few days before. It was not an ordinary storm, even for a groaning planet that had served up calamities for a hundred years or more. These thoughts flickered through her as she tried to stay awake, coiled upside down in a bag slung over Rilke's shoulder.

The journey to where Rilke lived was a hazy mishmash of

repetitive movement, and she perceived it in dreamy packets she couldn't make sense of. The sway of her weight in the sack, combined with the bounce she made against his side was hypnotizing.

In other moments she thought of the yacht's sickening motion during the first week they were on board. The cruise was still an adventure looming in Canto's imagination and she was excited as well, eager to see the promised views of submerged cities that were now ruins. It was a testament to the melt of ice, the last glacier gone and mourned nearly a century before.

Had she only known, she would not have wanted to see the coastal cities. She now had a taste of the fear and havoc the climate could wreak in a place like this. Her memory would forever be blurred by the sounds of that evening amid the lights and ringing bells. The tipping of the vessel first one way then the other, as well as the horrified screams. Others were down in the hull when the boat had collided with something submerged, invisible.

But the more she pressed to remember, the tighter the memory drew around her and blurred. These cities now reminded her of carcasses through some other memory of wildness, inherited from some strain of animal that slept deep within her. Or was it an embedded memory? She could not know.

Floating in and out of time, she was suddenly lifted, the analogue of a carnival ride she had once taken, a wheel that went up and around continuously. The lights had been strewn across the botanical gardens below where she had curled close to Canto and he had held her, reassuring her that she was safe. Then, she had buried her shimmering face into the crook of his arm for comfort.

For hours she slept and there were no more memories to

trouble her with what had been or what was to come. She heard through her dreams the sound of poetry, and it buoyed her up through the night's feverish and convoluted horrors. She would survive and perhaps she would even make it back home. Perhaps Canto was safe too.

The fox slept deeply when Rilke went to work the next day. He hurried through his deliveries, eager to return home.

Kasim raised his eyebrows when Rilke had held open the bag, exposing the silvery powder inside. But the baker shoveled the bagged loaves in without a word, counting them by twos. Then Kasim watched him disappear through the door faster than he'd ever seen him move.

Rilke's mind lingered on the strange being he had found washed up near the overpass. Had he known she slept peacefully all day, he would not have hurried less. The fox was beginning to stir just as Rilke came through the heavy door which opened into the house. He came into the room where she rested with his book tucked under his arm. At first he stared in amazement, as if he had doubted she would still be there. But then he proceeded in, and seated himself on the floor a few feet away. She had not touched the bits of bread he had left her, but the water was nearly gone. He moved as if to stand up but she narrowed her eyes.

"Not yet. Meet you." Even the way her thought transmitted to him communicated tiredness. Dumbstruck, he leaned back and placed his book in his lap. He studied her face, and her amber eyes appeared almost green in the dim light of evening. Had they changed, he wondered?

Fen regarded him cautiously, and he almost heard her other questions, the ones she wouldn't allow herself to project. He could tell she was unimpressed by his room in the way she held herself partly off the floor, forepaws primly crossed. Perhaps she also didn't think much of him, the way most people felt when they opened their doors for his deliveries. A shadow of contempt, along with poorly-withheld judgment, usually danced across their faces. It was unclear what Fen meant by "meet" so he studied the book in his hands.

Fen determined that this human lacked the material resources of Canto, but was still her only chance to get home. Her heart panged as she thought of home, and she noticed Rilke flinched as if in sympathy. She allowed her feelings to flow from her until Rilke could see all that she held back.

Canto was a gentleman, considerate of everyone. He dressed well, smelled nice, and had clean hands. He wore gloves when going out and liked to cook. They traveled together and she always had the finest views from the hotel windows, the airbus, the monorail. Wistful, her eyes narrowing, Fen glanced at Rilke and saw he was shuffling through the pages, feeling for something. She did not intend to hurt him with her remembering.

Rilke didn't know what to do with the image he now had in his mind of the life that Fen had lived. First, he wasn't accustomed to thinking of times and places separate from the one he inhabited. It was disorienting to be sitting in his room and also be hurtling through a shining city on a streak of light with people finely dressed, drinking bubbly juices out of tall crystal flutes with long stems. Then, there was also the matter of this man, and how pleasant he seemed through Fen's impressions. He seemed like the type of man who would politely decline a loaf of bread, but pay for it anyway, to give to someone else. He might even smile while doing so.

The world that Fen came from was so unlike the one Rilke had always known, that there was no comparison. He wanted to forget that she had shared this world with him through her mind, even in flashing seconds, but he found it was impossible. Worse, he suddenly felt an overwhelming desire to see all the things that she found familiar and to experience them, to explore her city, to travel on the edge of large windows and to look out at clear spaces with happy people and to smile without trying. Yearning was a painful new thing. For Rilke, such a future hurt him nearly as much as the past that caused Fen to pine.

Rilke chose a note that had been written on a blank page by hand. It was on old thin paper and he often studied it, more distracted by the lettering than the words themselves, which bore no name. But he had studied it many nights, puzzling over what it could describe. His reading on this evening emerged from him with a new urgency, for the sake of his guest and the intensity of her listening. The sentences pierced the soft dark of the room with a bending light that wrapped into itself. The meanings shifted in his mind as he sounded the words, not quite knowing the sum of them:

> Emerging from a low shelter
> into the clear open spaces:
> The land lucent and liquid-bright;
> every dwelling and yard rejoiced,
> as if the dazzling feat
> was humbly strung in secret.
> And then we turned: look: before
> the lavish rain, a splendor of spent darknesses,
> with the flooding of those celestial rifts
> an all-seeing gate.
> Below, to the left, the lands were crystalline:
> solemn, in anticipation of evening,
> silent-mouthed, having drunk deeply,
> and with flowers boldly, towardly turned.

No one had ever read words as a gift to Fen, directly to her. She usually watched the transactions of human beings with the same drowsy-eyed indifference and only a mild curiosity for what they cared about or what made them laugh. She had always focused on what way they admired her so that she could improve. She was sometimes the object of conversations, but rarely the listening subject to whom another spoke.

Canto sometimes spoke to her, when all of the other people had left and they were alone. He told her stories about her ancestors, how they had lived brief lives on the outskirts; how they leaped high and then dove into the snow to catch mice which they crunched with their sharp teeth. He would scratch the ruff of her neck and she felt gratitude. But Fen was created to serve Canto and to care for him. It was unexpected when he helped her to feel better about herself.

Fen was aware that the Earth was much older than humans and foxes. She knew herself to be unique. But never had she heard words that made her hunger for yet another earth of feeling beyond her reach.

As Rilke read the words to Fen, he sensed her memories which at first flashed along so quickly that he couldn't make meaning of them. He saw a field, stretching down across a land with hills in the distance. On either side, the sky was indigo, heavy with rain. The grasses were also glistening with drops already fallen. He knew that he had never seen such a place, so it was a memory of hers, of green, sloping fields and small houses dotting the hills as far as the eye could see. There was the curving bow of colors that his uncle had once called *akansyèl,* with a tone of reverence. Joyfully, his ma had laughed at Afi, and said *arcoíris,* before popping his behind with her towel. It was the only time Rilke had ever seen his ma look at Afi with something like love, and Afi had smiled back at her with a happiness that felt years overdue.

But as for the field with the rainbow draped over it, he had no such images in his mind. Instead, there was just the city after a deluge. The rain and wind settling in for days. The streams of dust that swelled into tiny rivers that closed off entire streets. He stayed in during those times, when the surge siren would wail its song. But more often, several weeks would pass without rain and the only flowers were wild, dry, and brown. He didn't know which was better or worse. But he did know where he wished he could be, and what hope looked like. It was now this field that stretched into infinitude, and trees that rimmed the sky's sinking light.

Fen saw that Rilke was studying her thoughts and learning how to communicate with her. Her entry to his mind was closed in several places. There were fewer shared images between them, but enough to create the opening which could lead to friendship.

"I want to see that place," Rilke blurted, in surprise at his own voice.

This reaction went well beyond what Fen could have expected. When she pressed, she could feel his surety, an unyielding premonition of adventure, much like what Canto had felt when he had planned their trip along the southern coasts of North America. As a Canadian, he thought of the South as an exotic locale, rife with rich foods and culture utterly unlike their home in Edmonton. Rilke's excitement reminded Fen of how she had felt then, too, before everything had gone wrong.

She tucked her snout into her paws and Rilke regarded her, unsure. Carefully he extended his hand to her shoulder and felt the thrill of her fur against his fingers. The powder lightly clung to his hand afterward, and fell onto the book in his hands. Unaccustomed to reassuring anyone but himself, he didn't know what to say.

"I don't know where it is," she countered.

This recognition was new to Fen, as was her hesitation. She had never turned away from travel, but she knew travel would not be the same with Rilke. There would be no window seats or full service sleeping compartments. She felt no desire to venture out into an unknown world without the protections Canto had provided. Rilke had no awareness of what such a journey entailed. Fen was careful to not let him discover these thoughts, the ones that said "no" to his wish which still hung in the air like the sound of a plucked string.

"It is a longer journey than you can imagine," she added.

She herself could not fathom the distance, much less summon the belief that she could find her way back home to Canada.

Unbidden, and without any act on his part, Rilke spoke words he meant, but were not his own.

"That which one was, to no longer be *that*, but to relinquish one's own name like a broken toy."

Fen tilted her face toward him with curiosity.

"What is it about the poet's words that makes you recall them?"

She saw the language turn in his mind like jewels and the jewels opened like the petals of a flower. She had not seen this steady unfolding happen so readily in another person before, besides Canto. Many of the people she observed had already decided the meanings of their words.

Rilke was open to images that arrived through her, unpronounced. The words were keys made to fit the organic circuitry of their minds. Her experiences formed sense impressions that she transmitted directly to him, and in his charged and receptive consciousness, he received her memories into his heart as feelings, and then finally as words.

She allowed him to see the rest of what she held back. Her racing heart, the terror of the wind and of the hurricane. He could almost smell the salt of the gyrating currents and feel the swells of water lifting the raft up several meters before drawing it down again into a sucking trough . . . the tumble, the force with which the raft rolled across an uneven shore littered with junk. The fox had dragged herself from the jagged waterline and had found the small alcove in the bank to rest. From there, the vision was mired in emotion and fear and went dark. Days must have passed without her awareness.

"I'm sorry that happened to you, Fen." He touched the top of her paw in sympathy, and her breathing gradually returned to normal. She resumed her aloof pose for just a moment, then relaxed and nosed the pieces of bread he had left out for her that morning. As she ate, he admired her beauty, and this rapidly formed into an alarming and fierce desire to protect her, to shield her from feeling afraid and alone like that again. In this way, they formed a language, and through this shared lexicon of fear and desire, they formed a plan to leave the city.

Rilke knew right away that Fen would refuse to ride in the bag.

Fen's large, angular ears flattened against her head and she pretended she could not understand his every thought. He didn't need to know her thoughts, given the sound erupting from her quarreling form. But when she paced forward and backward a few times and then sat back down, he knew that she recognized the dangers of traveling through the early morning streets exposed.

They had discussed the trip multiple times and she knew

that she must be carried in his delivery sack until they were safe. Fen recognized that she had lived her entire life in protected comfort. In moments, she permitted herself to think of her former life. She also considered the uncertainty that anyone else had survived. But then she would shake the thoughts away and concentrate on the task at hand.

"I don't like the smell inside that sack. It's moldy."

Rilke smiled weakly and looked down at the coin in his hands. All his labor, the years spent delivering loaves and parcels while living in his little room were distilled in the heavy metal chip. There was a figure with a huge backpack and mountains behind him on the chip. It was not money, because Rilke had never seen it before. He had a few credits too, but this coin represented something entirely different.

At first, he had imagined that they would have enough to board a train headed west through the tomato fields, perhaps even reaching the other side of them before they would have to begin walking. From there, he and Fen would set out on foot with a few days of concentrate foods and water. It hadn't been a plan with any solid parts except the moment when Fen wouldn't have to lie still in the bag as he carried her.

But Kasim had intervened when Rilke had explained he was leaving and needed to cash in his wage credits.

"Hey, Brother! You take this too. Much more valuable."

He pressed the heavy coin into Rilke's palm and closed his hand around it.

"You'll be safer. The train goes far and you walk with other people, okay?"

Kasim always looked right into Rilke with a sincerity and kindness that disarmed him. Kasim nodded toward the sack on Rilke's shoulder.

"That's all you have?"

For a second, Rilke froze, suddenly worried that Kasim

knew about Fen. But no, he was concerned about the integrity of the bag over the long journey. Kasim asked Rilke to wait, and returned with a tall, worn backpack from his office.

"You need this. No roof? Keep your clothes dry."

Kasim took it outside and beat it with a rolling pin for a few minutes. He coughed a little when clouds of flour shrouded his baker's hands and floated in the light.

It was a simple gesture, but Rilke had taken the dusty bag with thanks. Kasim's face softened and he rested his hands on the counter,

"When I was young, I traveled to see my sister in Atlanta. This bag was all I had. You'll be fine, Brother."

With that, he thumped the counter and walked back toward the ovens. Rilke clutched the bag gratefully and walked out of the bakery for the last time.

That had been a few hours before, and the reality was finally settling in that he was leaving. He was saying goodbye to the tiny brick bungalow and his life as a carrier of goods.

The fox wasn't insensitive to the pains he was taking to keep her safe. She was still vulnerable to the attention of others, even from inside the sack. Their best chance was to get out of the city unnoticed, and a little before dawn. She also knew how limited Rilke's resources were and what security he was leaving behind.

She watched him fold his few possessions into a tight square of cloth and slide it into a large pack with cushioned straps for his shoulders. The pack had been repaired many times. Rilke's book fit neatly into the outer pocket of a small courier bag he had brought from the stadium when he had left it years ago. He hadn't any other possessions to speak of, so there was nothing left to do but leave once Fen agreed to enter the sack.

"It's only until we are out of view. We may even have

most of the boxcar to ourselves."

Fen winced when he said "boxcar." She had accepted the repugnant idea that they might not have seats or a window, but she still struggled to be excited about this train journey which was so unlike the others she had taken before. They would probably travel with freight, and would move with painstaking slowness away from the coast. As freight, they would be traveling the way trains had continued in the South long past the advancements made elsewhere on the continent.

Fen recalled Canto's discussions that took place in pristine telecom rooms and in his Edmonton office. His company handled logistics for cross-continental travel, and she often dozed in and out of long quarterly reports in the background, as well as arguments about resources. She thought about these costs now while contemplating their trip overland. For someone like Rilke, who had only ever walked, rail would be exciting no matter how one traveled. He didn't need the luxury of Canto's life for it to be better and more enticing than the world he lived in now. And, she reasoned, riding along being carried by Rilke wouldn't be so bad.

She glanced at Rilke and knew that he had understood all of this, including her continuing distaste for traveling in a boxcar, in a moldy bakery sack, for an indefinite amount of time.

"How about the pack, then? There's room for you there, but it might be hard to breathe sometimes"

Fen sighed. Nothing about this would be easy. He lowered the pack to the floor and she burrowed in. Fen curled into herself as he gently tilted the pack upright. She managed to find a tiny seam where her nose could take in air. The air told her much about her environment, and she seemed pleased by it.

"Ready," she thought.

Rilke hoisted the pack onto his shoulders as gingerly as he could, careful to not disturb the fox inside. He pulled the door to, hearing the lock click behind him. There was no turning back now.

Rilke liked the silence when Fen wasn't talking, but instead remembering her life and reflecting on her existence. He was fascinated by the way her mind turned objects and sense impressions many different ways in her mind before setting them down again.

She knew that he listened and it was this comfortable way they had of thinking together that finally helped him understand small things at first and then larger things. Understanding that there were people somewhere in the world who could make a being like Fen made him hopeful that they were wise. He enjoyed the images of Canto which she frequently returned to. And occasionally, he detected a kind of delight she felt whenever she allowed herself to imagine seeing him again.

Rilke smiled at this thought, glad that she was finally positive about the journey ahead of them, as daunting as it was. He trudged out into the early morning streets nurturing his first hopeful thought that there might be a place for him in this new world of the north.

Kasim had told him to walk a short distance east until he came to the old railway and to turn right, walking south along the tracks. Rilke had thought to himself that walking east and then south in order to go north made no sense, but Fen had explained that sometimes a trip was twisty at the beginning before straightening out.

He accepted this answer, but then there was the matter of the ancient rail bed itself which offered him no confidence for what the tracks looked like elsewhere. In one segment, the marsh on both sides was almost level with his path, even though it had been raised as a part of the city's resilience program a hundred years before. At the first track intersection he was to go right, walking north, until he arrived at the historic overpass. Then the train station would be nearby.

He didn't expect to encounter anyone and he didn't, thankful that he lived on the side of the city that had already been given up. From what Fen knew, he managed to learn that all of the people who could leave had left already.

The dawn was on his right as he walked and Rilke realized that Fen had fallen asleep. He continued to think about the way ahead and all the things his city had forgotten to tell him about the world which he had learned from Fen.

Rilke cried. He couldn't help it, and he didn't remember the last time he had felt this way, or if ever at all. It was a loss far greater than any he had known because he had never lost anything of value that he knew of. Even leaving his family had been a gain in his happiness, if one could call it that. He was happier working for Kasim than he was hunting with Afi. He had done what his ma wanted him to do, which was move, move, move.

He struggled to remember the hard face of his ma and how tired and angry she always seemed. It was easier to remember his uncle, since his uncle had always seemed at peace on the boat. He was not sure if anyone else in the stadium had known his birth name or if he was seen any differently by them than anyone outside. None of it mattered anymore. He had not lived in the stadium for years, not since his ma gave him a coin and told him to leave and never come back. She said the next storm would be bad, and he needed to go before the stadium was cut off from the rest of the city. He hadn't wanted to, but then she had turned angry and drove him away by throwing rocks. They cried and screamed at each other, and that hurt far worse than the rocks ever could.

But he would not "count the old bad things all night long," as Rilke wrote in the eighth sonnet, but would instead "hold up the constellation of his thoughts to the sky, unclouded by breath." Everything that was good about his early life remained in his heart, even after he had left his first home in the stadium. Why not this, too?

When Rilke's ma had forced him to leave the stadium, it was because she had heard that the next year of floods would cut them apart from the rest of the city. He had begun walking north and west, lit by a dawn like this one, following 52nd across the last bridge to be built in the old part of the city. By the late morning on that day so many long years before, he had found Kasim's bakery. He bought a loaf of bread with the coin his ma had given him, and was given a job almost immediately. The old man had seen the desperation and the fear on the face of the young kid, but more importantly, he was down one courier and his cousin had a room to rent.

Rilke trudged along allowing his thoughts to wander even further away, in a timeless realm where all things past were also present and future.

According to his uncle, some people believed there had once been a child of the gods, a wise and beautiful being who had come to walk the Earth with humans and determine whether another hundred years would bring sorrow or illumination. The child was born into a home where no one showed it love and the indifference of the adults turned into a canker of neglect. This neglect grew into a great wound and all the pestilences of the world came to feed on it. Then they laid their eggs.

First hunger came, and then the fevers came, and then the houses could not protect against water or insects. The fish died. The forests became deserts and the rains moved unpredictably. The wound of the child swelled until the child was filled with infection and died. Many children died across the planet and generations called it the first sign of a forgotten future, the second being when children stopped being born at all. People said it was because there was no future. Others said it was the slumber of a world that needed to sleep. A silence fell like snow on a generation.

Without a future, in such a quiet world, why would any child choose to be born?

Once again, Fen endured the swing, the bump, the bounce, the rebounding method of travel by shouldered sack, but this time in a more balanced way. Whereas before, the sack had been a comfort after the terrifying hours spent huddled alone on the water bank, now it was a torment of repetition. It jogged another memory, one that she had already forgotten because of the now-central trauma of her life. Floating in a raft all night alone in the dark.

She did not remember how she had gotten there, only that she had trembled with the shock of it all. Once on the raft she had curled herself small to fit in the area under the seat. But then there was water and she had to sit up and fight to stay in the raft. There were no oars, useless to her. Had there been a human, they would have floated hours adrift just the same.

She could not remember the minutes before the water and wind came. She did not know if hours passed or days. She did not know if Canto had placed her in the boat before leaving her to help others, which is something he would have done, or if she herself had run across the tilting deck to press the signals to deploy the raft. Fen had the memories of different species in her, and all of them wanted to live.

Humankind's fascination with domestic animals and artificial intelligence had led to her, an enhanced lifeform, to be custom designed according to the preferences of the contract buyer. Once the order was finalized, her programming began. It was no secret, what she was. Adaptable, as her ancestors had been, and clever.

Hyperactivity and wildness were edited from her genome. Her lifespan was increased. The chitin was a bizarre modification that Mimi had selected because Canto had always loved butterflies when he was a child. The protein-laden powder they left on his fingertips had mesmerized him.

Canto cried when Mimi first explained that he should not touch them, that their wings were too fragile to touch and they might die. He had fallen ill shortly after, and the doctor had said he was susceptible to guilt. Mimi had known then what kind of hope he desperately needed.

It was midmorning when Rilke arrived at the station and saw two trains rumbling on the nearest tracks. The ramp had seen better days, perhaps when people were deciding to leave the city for good. Fen wriggled a little to show she was awake and yawned inside the stuffy pack.

"Are we there yet?"

"Nearly. I need to find the conductor."

Kasim had told him to find the blue door with the window and present the special coin. Kasim had this coin for years but never used it. Rilke wondered for a moment. Kasim was cheerful when he came into his shop in the mornings. "We're feeding people, my brothers!" he would shout as he fired up his ovens. The couriers and the bakers all speculated that Kasim did not sleep. Other people said he was waiting on someone and spent his nights in prayer. Any day could bring that hoped-for reunion.

Dream

The fox must have known her name first. *But no.*

She was the best of hybrids, configured to live longer and without the diseases common to her ancestors. Mods like empathy pins and comfort scripts were benefits the wealthy paid extra for. She knew what she had, she knew what to be, but she didn't know what any of it meant. She wanted to understand.

Her value to someone like Canto was immeasurable given that she was every cat or dog he had ever loved. They were all there, buried in her design like layers of an ancient city. Her memories were theirs and all of them remembered Canto, wanted his pat, his glance, his approval. Or to catch the ball, to follow the string, to dig in the earth.

The Earth.

Once, she had wondered about these thoughts while resting her head in the lap of Canto's grandmother, an elegant and smooth-faced woman with cloudy eyes and silver hair that ballooned into a loose and magnificent bun. Pearls dripped from her ears and the fox desperately wanted to bat them, or even take them away somewhere and bury them, to protect them, and also to protect herself.

"What am I?"

The elderly woman had continued to stroke the fox's head and along her back, slowly to the end of her voluminous tail before returning to the fox's snout with one jeweled finger. Then she traced the route again with a warm open palm. All this with no regard to the luminescent chitin that collected on her soft hands.

"You are special, my dear. You are an archive of affection and hope."

The elder-woman's hand glimmered in the light but she paid it no mind, staring straight ahead. Mimi always seemed youthful and mischievous, though her back was bent, and she sometimes fell asleep spontaneously.

"Mimi, what am I to you?"

The woman pondered the images as they surfaced in Fen's consciousness until she saw herself pictured there as well: A porch, a green field parting before a quivering nose; the ecstasy of slipping into a tiny heated burrow and curling into herself for a nap; someone scratching under a twitching chin, one feline paw outstretched; the memory of a younger Mimi pulling on her gloves, leaving for the opera.

"Mimi, what am I to Canto?"

These were the questions that remained unanswered though there were glimpses of recognition from one set of eyes and then another. This fleeting recovery was all there had ever been.

Leaving Savannah

Rilke smiled to himself as the sun cast a beam of light across the changing morning. He was supposed to begin near the falls. The trail was the best way to travel north, according to Kasim, because walking through the mountains would be much safer than the roads and towns. There would be water, and most of it drinkable.

The short man behind the blue door was helping a woman when Rilke approached. She was thin and smartly dressed. She wore a plumed hat with at least two kinds of flowers. Beside her stood a large trunk, nearly twice as large as she was. The woman smelled nicer than anyone Rilke had ever encountered and yet she had the same expectant air about her that people in the stadium did. It was the anxiety of living in an old city with many kinds of people, some of them new. He heard her curt remark to the conductor's question—"Richmond!"—and quickly, another porter came to roll her bag to the train and load it. The click of her heels as she walked away signaled wealth, and this was Rilke's first real introduction.

When Rilke reached the ticket window he placed the medallion on the worn counter with a metallic snap and looked at the man who wore a navy cap and a wizened expression. The man's white mustache twitched once when the kid said "Gainesville."

The old man studied the youth then studied the coin and began to punch some numbers into a strange machine. It wasn't like the one that Kasim had in his shop, but it was similar. It spat out a small chit of paper and he handed it to Rilke.

"You will be riding on a different train than that lady that was here before. Some folks would say that she has the better seat, and therefore will enjoy her trip more. But you have something better."

Here he held up the coin with a smile. "This is the beginning of a new life."

He held the coin tilted in the light and showed Rilke a number that had been buried in the detail of a mountain.

"This coin was minted thirty years ago. I haven't seen one of these in a while."

Musing, he placed the coin in a special box and took from under the box a small paper pamphlet. Glossy images of people walking into the trees beside a waterfall shone on the brochure. The conductor opened the front panel and pointed to a name on the bottom of the page.

"Ask someone at the station how to find her. She can help you."

Rilke followed the man as he stepped from his counter, opened the door, and pointed down the platform to a green bench.

"I'll be there momentarily to let you into your cabin."

After the man returned to his counter, Rilke felt Fen shift her body again, signaling her impatience but also the possibilities that were awakened by the word *cabin*.

The train car was surprisingly clean and had at one time been used to transport whole families in each compartment, offering them two bench seats and a large square window. There was nothing fancy about the compartment he was directed to, but there was privacy, which Fen took advantage of immediately.

For a moment, Rilke decided that she looked happy, or as happy as a fox could appear without words. But then the words came, in his mind, a response to his unguarded thought.

"But you know I am happy. What would I be otherwise?"

He marveled at her light, shining form and the way her coat rippled in the breeze from the open window. He sat across from her, looking back toward Savannah. Water was all around them. The train began to gain momentum and creak and rock along the track. They were finally moving.

He thought of his ma and his uncle, all the people in the stadium, and wondered whether he would ever see them again. In other ways he was glad to not think of them again. It was an awkward, ambiguous feeling he couldn't sort out at first, until he thought back to a line of poetry.

"The sacred, frightened landscape, which you feel in farewells."

But no—it was before that. He opened his tattered book, careful with the pages.

> Here, falling
> is the most efficient way. From the skillful feeling
> of being overtaken, down into the intuited, further.

Fen had already circled into herself and was resting again, which worried him just a little. She seemed more irritated in her thoughts than before and they tended to skip a bit, swinging wildly between joy and fear.

As the sun mounted the sky and the train pulled out of the city, the tomato fields overtook everything in his view. He wondered about the people who worked them. Did they lead a better life than the people who had lived in the stadium? How could he know?

Fen was for the moment content, and she had lost everything that was important and safe to her. When he thought this, he heard the fox make a chittering whine in her sleep. Was she dreaming or listening?

Perhaps it was the brief moments of joy that joined the panels of a patchwork life. Maybe, had he tried to leave the city years ago, he wouldn't have earned Kasim's generosity. After all, Kasim had the coin for years and had never used it. But here Rilke was, hurtling along a track and gaining speed, on his way to the mountain path.

When they were boarding the train, Rilke had looked back toward the eastern skyline, toward the sea, which had always been both prod and obstacle, a retribution for centuries of negligence. What had any of them done to deserve this? What had brought this on the city and the people living there?

But here, the joy again, threading through his worry and filling it with light.

Just before boarding, the conductor had looked at the kid expectantly, his mustache twitching once or twice when he asked for a name. When the kid said "Rilke," the conductor had written something on a small clipboard and then held out his hand.

Without knowing for sure what it meant, Rilke reached out and grasped the man's hand which was warm and dry.

"Good luck, young Rilke," said the conductor, and the kid felt a surge of confidence from hearing his chosen name spoken aloud.

Fen had communicated nothing for a moment, happy enough to shake herself free of the pack and take in the air fully once they were in the train compartment. After the train began to move she turned toward him and sent forward a sleepy, warm thought. Tilting her head, she seemed to laugh with the thrill of travel.

Rilke grinned at her modestly and recited the first words of his new life and the last of his old one.

"When earthly things forget you, say to the still earth: I flow. To the rushing water say: I am."

Fen took in the sight of the youth, looking toward the city wistfully as the distance whittled it away. She was beginning to learn what Canto had meant when he had said he would always be with her.

Rilke watched the countryside pass through the window of the train as he traveled further from the coast. He was soothed by the repetitive click-clack as the wheels struck against the line. He was in and out of a doze, saying his new name to himself, recognizing and remembering how it felt to say "Rilke" aloud for the first time. He didn't recall any name before it, having lived in a world of strangers. Or, at least he felt that way when he thought about his ma and uncle.

Rilke was physically tired but mentally charged. He could name himself, leave the city of his youth and embark for the unknown. He had known no one, loved no one, but now he was Rilke and he had a friend who showed him a world through her mind that he could almost imagine.

The people in that world stared at themselves approvingly in tall mirrors unlike anything Rilke had ever seen, apart from the unbroken windows in the quiet districts closest to the water. He saw the mirrors and the people and the tall buildings with intact windows through the fox's memories and through her dreams.

But there were occasional partitions. These were places of Fen's mind that were closed to him.

She had begun to question her name. She was in doubt over more basic things too, like what had happened before he had discovered her, shivering and alone. Rilke's thoughts were increasingly about her but he worried. He noticed that she was growing steadily more tired though all she had done was sleep since they had boarded the train. He knew she was still shaken by being lost, so he didn't question her confusion when she occasionally pressed an idea forward and then retreated.

"Forest? No."

She would be half in and out of dreams and mumble, as if searching for something.

"Fen? No . . . Rainbow? Yes."

He observed her restless sleep and noted where her mind went, until it went places he could not follow, that were secret even to her. In other moments, he stared at the departing track. Sometimes he peeked out from another angle to see where it led. But most of the time he was more comfortable seeing where he had been.

The marsh stretched in all directions away from the shining track. Houses sat sometimes halfway in and out of water. Alligators sunned themselves on islanded patios and porches that had once been tended. Rilke imagined the reptiles as the new residents, swimming through doorways and into bedrooms, sleeping in beds of silt and sludge. The sounds of late summer stretched into October. He had known more summer than any other season. Like the gators, he felt sleepy and warm. He pressed his cheek against the window, continuing his reverie.

Rilke was learning that people traveled more than he had thought possible. He had not known anything but the inside of the stadium for most of his life. His was the crowded slum remaining on the edge of the flooded city. His people had stayed. They would not leave the coast though the signs of deluge and loss were everywhere. Ruin was written on the previous decades as well as the future. At least that's the way it seemed at first until Rilke began to notice the sun changing across different landscapes.

Even the idea of a landscape felt new. Cloud shadows skated leisurely across the fields. Words came to his lips unbidden.

"Grape gives way to vineyard, full on his voluptuous southern hills."

Rilke paused at the word *voluptuous*. He wasn't sure what it meant. But it sounded like it asked many soft questions, like grapes sometimes did. Would the taste be sour? Or sweet?

At the sound of his voice, the fox had stirred a little, and Rilke smiled as he imagined her dreaming of fruit-draped slopes, which he saw hazily through her memories of them. Green garlands drooped along the hills in places Rilke could only see because Fen had seen them herself. He liked this new way of knowing and seeing. He hoped that he might eventually see these places too.

The track they traveled across wound its way inland. Old freight lines became new passenger lines because steel was what persisted when everything was scavenged and melted down. Only the determined, newly-arrived migrants found relief in these old towns from whatever they had witnessed before. Most stayed, which spoke the loudest about whatever they were fleeing from.

Rilke knew none of this history. He only knew that some people had never left the city once they got there and his ma was one of those. She had come from further west but had finally let go of her nomadic push north. This was because she had met Rilke's Uncle Afi. He was the one who suggested going east before going north. He knew of a place where the tides, fickle and profound, would periodically take everything away, but leave far more in return. They could scavenge in Savannah. He said he only needed a boat to make it, and by that time she was pregnant with Rilke, her savings gone.

Life was hard and had always been, said his ma. The limited choices that people made rarely resulted in a better life, just more of it. Another day to spend hustling and bartering, scrapping and sorting. This was his ma's perspective.

Rilke shook away a sense of unfairness, and focused his eyes on the boggy ground giving way to hilly ditches and crops he didn't recognize. He wished Fen would wake up and tell him what flashed by through his window, but she slumbered on.

Rilke had been fully asleep, his face pressed against the glass of the compartment. He was unaware that the pack where the fox slept had come open and her own drowsing form was partially visible. Warm and relaxed, he was shaken awake by the weighted and screeching shiver of the train.

"We're stopping," thought Fen.

Rilke wiped his drool on his sleeve, looked groggily about and rearranged the lid of his knapsack so the fox was once again concealed. The afternoon was coming in and the emboldened light cast a glow over the edge of what appeared to be a town. A sign read WADLEY and had just cleared the frame of the window as the train finally ground to a halt. A light knock on the door, then a voice. The train would be taking on mail and additional passengers.

In a fit of nervousness, Rilke reached for his courier bag and withdrew his only book. He had been accustomed to reading aloud during nights when the storms buffeted his city and during afternoons when he had felt similarly uneasy. He sometimes felt this way, even when the skies were clear. When he was sad he read and remembered attachments to people and objects and feelings past. Here was something new, though. He did not know why he felt panic, or why he reached for the beaten paperback other than out of habit.

Outside the compartment, he heard the rhythmic shuffle of feet, moving slowly in unison. His active imagination was suddenly awake to possibilities he had never considered before.

Rilke began to read to himself the familiar, scriptural lines. It soothed him, and he remembered the isolated world of the stadium. Then his mind went to the things he recalled in deep memory. There had been an old car seat that his uncle had found. It sat in front of his ma's place, built of cardboard and shore-found flotsam. But Rilke was not in the stadium anymore, nor was he on the train when he began to read from his book:

> Like a strange boy whom one endlessly allows to play,
> but who cannot catch the ball
> and can play none of the games
> which the others play so easily with one another,
> but stands there and looks away, but to what?

> I suddenly stood,
> realized that you were toying with me.

Sometimes Rilke felt that *this* Rilke, the poet whose words he read aloud every day to calm himself and feel less lonely, had understood how he himself felt at times.

Rilke shook his head and stopped. How could anyone know how it felt to be him or how narrow the walls around him had seemed, or how predatory the city had sometimes felt? It was his feelings that he assumed to be his weakness. He could not easily contain his fear and it stalked him. Though he had been alone, he wondered what it could mean now to have a friend.

Just as Rilke began to read again, the door opened.

Rilke was startled when a smartly dressed woman in her mid-twenties leaned inside the door.

"Do you mind if I join you?" she asked. Her shiny bright hair lay straight and smooth past her shoulders. Her eyes were an uncommon blue, and she appeared to look through Rilke in polite scrutiny. Feeling rude, he turned shyly away, answering with a nod and his own greeting. He spoke softly, angling his head down to look back at his book. He glanced over at her as she sunk wearily into the seat diagonally from him and adjusted her cases. She had been in the sun. Rilke had seen this once before and tried not to stare. She was still getting settled and unpacking a few things in the seat next to her. They were shapely oblong squares that reflected light, stacked magnetically, and looked expensive.

Not knowing what else to do or say, Rilke began to read again, but this time to himself.

The woman finally stopped and looked at him. He hoped she would not leave but he also felt protective of Fen. What if the fox moved or woke up?

Under the woman's gaze, Rilke looked out the window as he closed the book.

"What are you reading?"

It seemed she really meant the question, so he held his book up for her to see.

"I haven't read much of his work. But I like poetry from the twenty-first century." The woman shaped the words in a way much different from how he spoke and the people he had known. She was deliberate and careful, and her words seemed to emerge from the front of her mouth. Her voice was also soft, ending with a question's upward lilt, even when she wasn't asking a question.

Rilke shifted in his seat. "So you read too?"

She nodded. "I am a reader, yes. And do you read books other than poetry?"

Rilke had to think for a moment, as he didn't know how to characterize the kind of reading he did. He was taught reading in school but it was only after he had found the book of Rilke's poetry that he came to own a book himself and chose to read it.

"Only this book," he lifted it up and one of the pages drifted out, falling awkwardly toward the bag where Fen hid quietly. He rapidly retrieved it and put the page back in place with precise care. He was relieved that she seemed patient. Sometimes his teachers at the annex had not been.

"And what is your name?" She pulled her golden hair back into a messy coil and secured it.

How should he say his name to her when he had named himself after the poet?

"It's who you are, Rilke," offered the fox with a mental shrug. Fen knew where his mind was sliding: back into the dark, stalked corners of the past where he doubted himself and any future he could have elsewhere. He inhaled deeply before saying his name and spoke hesitantly.

"My name is Rilke." Then, as a shy afterthought, "Like the poet."

The woman accepted his answer with a nod and another smile.

"And my name is Brynja." She sat back into the seat with some tiredness and he noticed she had kicked her shoes off. They were expensive and made from a material he had never seen before. He saw that she was being genuine, but that she was also distracted. He also realized a horrific odor was filling the car. Was it her feet? Fen chuckled to herself and Rilke cleared his throat loudly to cover the sound.

It was clear that speaking took more of Brynja's time than she preferred. He could tell this about people and had seen it whenever he had sometimes disturbed Kasim after a work shift. His former boss would answer Rilke's questions but then turn back to his console where he fed numbers and sighed or scratched his head in exasperation.

Rilke could see that it was like that with her too, but she kept it hidden. Rilke felt that Brynja's work had something to do with the stack of panels in the seat next to her because her attention went back to them and the smile disappeared from her mouth for just a second. Then, as if she realized how transparent she'd suddenly become, the smile was back.

"Are you hungry?" She spoke breathlessly, as if she had found one more opportunity to delay something inevitable and unpleasant.

When he glanced nervously at the sack, thinking of the fox concealed within, she interjected, misreading his gesture. "No, allow me."

Before he could refuse, she placed her index finger in front of her ear and spoke in a monotone, the way he had seen Kasim do when navigating the bakery's network.

"Concessions."

In what felt like a few seconds, there was a brisk knock at the compartment door. Brynja leaned forward to open it and a young girl with braids entered carrying a metal box on each hip and a tablet on her belt. He had seen these before, when people sold meat sticks at the winter market, once when he was young. The meat was usually gator. They had taken over the barrier islands and were plentiful, which is why Afi always had work as a hunter.

"Hi, Tammi." said Brynja. She drew her hand downward in front of her stomach reflexively and that was when Rilke noticed she was communicating with her hands, The gestures continued between the two and in moments the girl had reached into one of the boxes on her hip and drew out two skewers with grilled squash, onion, and cornmeal-breaded chunks of protein.

Then Brynja said "Sweets?" while drawing her hand down twice after brushing her stomach again. Fascinated, Rilke watched how comfortably the two passed information between them.

Tammi smiled impishly before reaching into one of the boxes where she withdrew fresh roasted figs, also on skewers. The plump pink interiors stood out against their green skins.

Rilke was still marveling at their beauty when Brynja handed him one of each. He was sure his eyes betrayed his wonder. In his excitement he almost missed seeing that Tammi discreetly nodded toward his pack while signaling to Brynja. Rilke's attention turned immediately to the food, sure that the exchange had been something he had only imagined.

Brynja glanced at the massive pack, nodded, and waved in an arc downward from her mouth, the back of her hand flashing for a second before her index touched her ear once more. "Tip forty percent."

Tammi glanced at her tablet with a huge grin and gave a brief wave before disappearing from the cabin.

Fen knew Rilke was nervous but communicating with him was too risky. He had nothing more than a souvenir brochure in his pocket and a few coins. How would Brynja understand the trip he was making without also knowing about Fen?

Even the conductor had seemed in awe when presented with the old token at the station. And when he had told Rilke to find the woman in Gainesville, the fox had shivered at the uncertainty of finding someone they didn't know in a place they didn't know either. Now the fox felt more tired than usual, and her thoughts kept knitting and unraveling, despite her efforts to stay alert and vigilant.

Canto would never have traveled with so many things left undecided. She recalled his dark eyes and his musical voice. He could ask people to do things for him in a way that made them want to. Everyone wanted to please Canto. When she would ask Canto about it, he stroked her head and told her that they wanted something he continually gave away.

She missed that circle Canto always drew around them, at the same time she was learning to appreciate Rilke's innocence. He was like her, having seen very little of the world. But just as Canto's orbit induced people to care for him, the circle that Rilke cast around him had a similar effect, but for different reasons. Every moment felt like a continuation of their first encounter, when she knew she could trust him and he would help her.

The influence Rilke had was natural and she knew other humans could sense that. She could hear their heart beats sometimes, and could faintly gauge the pulses of their interiors. But this woman, the one charming Rilke with food, had a power the fox sensed with foreboding. Though the woman was talking about her home in Hafnarfjörður, she was also studying Rilke with an intensity that the fox could feel through her sluggish state and the pack that engulfed her.

Fen also felt studied, even as the woman seemed to laugh and delight in Rilke's stories. Rilke described not knowing how to eat the food that Kasim sometimes prepared in the bakery. He had never seen anything like *msakhan* before, since they only ate gumbo or stew in the stadium where he lived.

Even from the blind darkness of the pack, the fox knew that the woman's face had tightened and her smile had disappeared.

"Why are you leaving the city that you've known all your life?"

Rilke stopped chewing and considered his answer.

"Speak true," thought the fox, with a kind of resigned urgency. She was beginning to fail, her ideas slurring together into vague impressions.

"I'm taking my friend home. To where she belongs." He said this without fear or alarm, comforted by the meal they were eating together and the conversation that came so easily.

As her focus began to fade in and out, Fen decided there was no use to pretend. At least Brynja would know Rilke wasn't alone and that he was telling the truth.

Fen felt the sharp pang of what she had been feeling at first as a dull ache, now grown into a burning net of pulsing shocks. It pulled at her eyes and ears, and even her nose. What part was her? And where was the hurt? She could no longer tell.

"Who is your friend?" Brynja asked with a new edge to

her voice.

Rilke was taken slightly off-guard. "She's sleeping," he said quietly as he nodded toward the bag.

"She's an animal, then?" He saw Brynja begin to slide her hand toward the inside of her jacket and he instinctively knew he should remain still.

"Yes, but she is different. I don't think she is used to being lost."

The fox felt the wave of empathy roll forward from Brynja, which was the hoped-for response, but also underscored the questions that were not being asked. The fox was careful not to think them by accident.

But Rilke had told Brynja the truth from the first moment, and she could see that. Every city held many more like him, and if not exactly like him, more desperate and dangerous. He did not seem like that kind. Still, she made caution a habit.

"May I meet your friend?" Brynja had pulled a narrow tool from an inner pocket and it lit up in her hand as she rested it discreetly by her side.

The fox knew it was her responsibility to help Rilke and to explain what she was able to through him. She poked one trembling whisker out of the sack's mouth and her nostrils expanded with the strange and wondrous scents of the food, of the cabin, and Brynja's feet.

When she saw Fen, Brynja gasped and her eyes lit up.

Brynja

Fen saw how Brynja looked at her and peered back fiercely. Her amber eyes flashed with tinges of indigo, and they surveyed the woman with an equal measure of cunning and protectiveness.

"This human is my friend and guardian."

"I do not mean either of you harm," Brynja said slowly with a curious and calming air. Trying to be inconspicuous, she slipped the narrow object back into her coat pocket.

Rilke glanced quickly in surprise at Fen, realizing the two of them could communicate without his help. The fox managed a weak smile which he felt without actually seeing.

"What Rilke says is true. He's helping me return home."

"Does he know what you are?"" Brynja raised a single eyebrow.

"I do not know myself," Fen thought, panting.

"I don't understand," said Rilke with some disappointment showing through.

57

Brynja reached out briefly and touched Fen's coat. The fox did not flinch, but allowed the touch.

"She is a remote intelligence unit. She's designed to observe wildlife, to gather data about the natural environment that can help scientists balance it. But her chromatophores have defaulted. She could be any color, even assume the appearance of her surroundings as a protective camouflage. But something's wrong."

Brynja's hands were coated in powdery, iridescent chitin. She wiped the pearlescent dust on a napkin and drove her point home by writing out the words on a slip of paper she drew from a small notebook beside her. Then she handed the note to Rilke.

"Remote Artificial Intelligence and Nature-Balancing Observational Wildlife," he read aloud. Then he saw the acronym. This explained why their first encounter was overlaid with the image of a rainbow, and why she had seemed to reflect every color in the sunlight the day he had found her. Since then, she had faded to a pale gray, though still radiant in certain moments.

Hearing these thoughts, the fox lowered her head, defeated and panting rapidly. Rilke felt increasingly brave and indignant, still taking in the concept of his friend across a divide that separated her from him, and even from herself. Words sometimes kept people from knowing who they were, his uncle often said.

Rilke turned to Brynja with a serious expression.

"I think Fen is herself and not a thing. You've hurt her." He looked at Fen whose eyes were closed. She was lying still. But faintly, he heard her response.

"Brynja not hurt. Fen breaking."

The fox rested on her paws, rapidly breathing, still halfway in the pack and partly out, head and neck stretched forward. Her eyes closed, once, twice, and then once again. She was failing.

Rilke's heart was gripped with fear. With a worried expression he stroked her head and ears and reached for his book.

"My ma said the most beautiful place she had ever been was the swamp."

"Like a fen?" asked the fox.

Rilke glanced questioningly at Brynja who nodded quickly.

"Yes, it was like a fen. But I could not see it so it did not exist. But she believed in it."

"Read," she asked.

Rilke began:

> Unsecured on the mountains of the heart.
> See how small there,
> you can see:
> the last village of words, and higher,
> but also, however small, one last
> steading of feeling. Do you know it?

In part to comfort himself, he continued, seeing for himself the high places where love might leave one stranded and alone, and also feeling them.

But the final lines consoled Rilke somehow. They formed the last of Fen's thoughts that she would remember from that moment. Later, when the other forgotten things had been recovered, she would be comforted by them again:

> Perhaps there are healing sentients,
> all around, the mountain creatures,
> who vary and linger. And the great fearless bird

circles around the summit in pure denial—But
vulnerable, here on the mountains of the heart.

Brynja nudged Rilke when she saw Fen stir. The two had
been reclining and playing cards, but now they both sat up
with interest.

There had been damage to one or two sectors of a kind
Brynja found familiar and easy to repair. Her thesis project
had been an augmented wildlife unit. She said this casually
as she removed one of the fox's pins to scan it, and Rilke's
dread finally gave way to relief.

Brynja gestured toward the fox's coat which had changed
from the pearly, prismatic sheen he had once believed to be
permanent. Brynja said she had needed to overwrite the
chitin programming, and one or two other mods had been
lost as result. But the fox would be more likely to blend in,
she added, and there would be fewer conflicts between her
organic base and her cybergenetic directory.

As if to demonstrate Brynja's point, the fox shaded into
brown, tipping into an even darker brown, and then red, and
finally a color that matched the mahogany seat where she lay
curled. For about an hour, she was nearly invisible as the
fibers in her coat expanded and shifted her pigments.

"Her ability to adapt is what keeps her safe," Brynja
whispered.

Rilke did not question Brynja after all that he had seen.
Brynja had warned that the fox might not be the same as
before, given that Fen's comfort script had been in conflict
with her observational protocols. Had Fen ever been given a
data objective? Did layers of memory keep her focused on
finding home? Or were human social environments the
primary field of her observations?

Rilke understood none of Brynja's muttered thoughts,

recognizing that she was talking to herself as she worked. Brynja had seen many kinds of applications and hacks, and had modded a few herself. All of Rilke's concerns dissolved when the fox's fur settled into a tawny cinnamon, and when after resting for about an hour, the fox rolled over in the seat and stretched. She snuffled a bit then placed her paws over her eyes. Her ear had flipped around which made her seem a little clownish. Rilke breathed out in relief.

"Rilke?" She yawned, her paws still over her eyes. "I'm going to sleep a little more."

At this, his heart fluttered with joy.

Brynja expressed worry over his and Fen's itinerary when he showed her the brochure.

"You're going to walk? To the processing center in Maine?" This was the first time that her accent seemed to disappear, and what she said as a question didn't sound like a question, but expression of disbelief.

He hadn't thought about it in those terms, only that he and Fen would be traveling for a long time, and walking was the only free way to get anywhere. The way she said "Maine" implied that the distance might be a factor worth considering.

"You know that it's October now. You can't walk the mountain path in the winter."

This was certainly something he had not considered and he was embarrassed each time she told him something important about the world he knew so little about.

"I'm just saying that you need to rethink this plan of yours. I know you want to help Fen, but she is responding to her homing protocols. Whatever she 'feels' could be a string of code. Or worse, the instinctual drive of a wild animal. Modified, but still unpredictable."

Whenever Brynja talked this way about Fen, Rilke looked

away. He didn't want to argue with her, especially since she had been so helpful and knew so much about Fen and what she had been designed to do. But when she said words like *feel* and *instinct* there was a coldness there that made him think about the gators he and his uncle watched from the illusory safety of the boat.

"They do not care about you. They only want you in their stomach! It is their nature to sleep until they must act. And they act out of instinct which is not the same as understanding. That is why we kill and eat them. Because they would do the same to us." Rilke's uncle always tried to make Rilke feel better about the hunting they did for the family. He could tell that Rilke had a soft heart and did not enjoy the moment when the bangstick was placed against the large reptile's skull and the seconds after. Whether the animal was dead or unconscious, Rilke always felt sick when the snout was secured and they heaved the animal into the boat. In Rilke's mind, he should not have to depend on the deaths of other creatures. But to his uncle, hunting was how they survived, how he provided for his family, and how he held his place in the stadium.

Rilke saw Fen differently than the animals he and his uncle harvested for food, but he felt like Brynja saw them all in the same category. For her they were material components to life in this world that was both larger and more confining than he had expected.

Did everyone think this way, in terms of credits and contracts? Of humans at the center and everything else along the periphery, as some kind of scaffolding? He had heard it said that life was a wheel because life spun forward and one was sometimes up or sometimes down in its movement. But now he saw the spokes of the wheel and humans at the center of those spokes. All other beings were at the outer edge, not holding on but being held, gripped by the need at the center of the human being, or perhaps only one human being. The one with the most power.

He had never felt himself to be at the center of things but at their edges, much like the animals and other people without influence. Fen was also there with him, on the spokes or at the edge, not at the center. Someone like Canto was sure to be in the middle, and perhaps also Brynja, though he had seen her show compassion to him and Fen. He could see that she was someone other people obeyed. For him, that kind of power was something he did not want for himself, though he also didn't want to spend his life along the spokes or at the edge. He didn't like seeing Fen there either. Perhaps neither mastery nor survival described how he saw the dimensions of his own life.

After two rounds of naps, the fox exhibited what Brynja called frenetic random activity. Fen hopped up into one seat and then the other, her tail spinning wildly. She was also preoccupied with her name and introducing herself. Sometimes she would jump from seat to seat, look in each of their faces to inspire belly rubs, then drive her snout along the floor of the compartment before curling back to bite the end of her long tail. This energy was surprising to Rilke who had only seen Fen drowsy and sad.

Every few minutes she would look one of them in the eyes and say "I am Fen!" before falling on her back and chattering her foxy laughter.

And then the cycle would begin again.

"Her default must be joyful play," Brynja said wryly while she shook Fen's growling mouth side-to-side and smiled. With a snort, the fox lay relaxedly across the seat with her paws in the air, belly exposed.

Brynja had traveled with Rilke and Fen for a few hours. Soon the stops became more frequent and prolonged. As the train neared Macon, the land began to change again. They were near the Fall Line, where the Atlantic Coastal Plain met the Piedmont.

By now, Brynja understood more about Rilke and Fen's journey, and why the fox had been hiding in the pack. It had been a good instinct on Rilke's part but a few things about how he saw the country outside of Savannah troubled her.

"So you just turned your house key over and left your job? Didn't you file an intent to leave the city? There are risks." When she spoke to him like this, he felt dumb and chastised, but he knew Brynja was just looking out for him. She saw the world much differently than he did. She saw dangers where he only saw adventure.

Rilke looked at his shoes, hand-me-downs from Kasim's cousin, feeling like he did the first days after he first began making deliveries. He didn't know that leaving the city was dangerous. He had spent the first part of his life in a place where Brynja would never have traveled. Daily he had walked through condemned areas where only squatters lived.

Also, he had been "You, Kid!" for the past five years. He was able to measure this time through the people he saw on his route. Sal put pictures on the door during different months and this is how Rilke kept track of the seasons. The gaunt old man took two loaves because his wife was sick and never came to the door. Rilke saw her once and she was weakly built, her cataract-covered left eye unseeing. Her hand shook on the doorknob as she reached for the bread.

One day she had been there and then Old Sal said it had been five years since she had come to the door. He had seemed touched by Rilke's asking about her but then the smile faded and he wished Rilke a good day. By those moments, the kid had marked time. That, and by his nightly readings from the bedraggled poetry book nestled in his courier bag.

But Brynja was trying to explain to Rilke that the world was not built in moments like those, but through technological advancements, treaties, and opened shipping lanes where Nordic and Russian ships poured like coins. Rilke wondered if there would always be elements of life outside of Savannah that he would never understand.

While Fen snored lightly in yet another nap, Brynja explained her work to Rilke. Brynja's recruiting was completely legal. The States had expanded human resource contracts after the northern sea lanes opened and the desert began to devour the Midwest.

"What would people do, otherwise, Rilke? What would you have done had you not met Fen?"

This was something he had not considered. He always imagined that eventually he might become a baker for Kasim.

At this answer, Brynja shook her head. "The world is much bigger than the one you have been living in." She fanned her cards across the foldout table, and four queens stared up at him with icy expressions.

Brynja tried to justify the work that she did by describing crimes in parts of the country where human potential lay untapped. It was people like her who found work for the unemployed and the indigent. Most people had nothing to lose by signing with a shipping company for a twenty year haul. It was a great pension, provided anyone survived the hard life that the shipping lanes demanded.

Workers also wanted the genetic corrections the companies provided as an added benefit. Editing often involved a life free of disease and the mental worries brought by poverty, even if it did result in infertility most of the time. Without contractors like her, she argued, crime would flourish unabated.

"But I still don't understand why some people are deleted," Editing made sense, because through it someone's life might be improved. They could be healed from a disease or given desirable attributes like immunity to illness or a longer lifespan. But deletion was permanent. It was death, however humane the delivery.

Brynja tried to help him see it differently. "There are some crimes that surpass passion. Some people are cruel and are not capable of feeling empathy. You wouldn't be able to imagine them unless you knew what evil human beings were capable of."

Rilke looked out the window again, noticing that the fields were dotted more heavily with shacks and occasional small farms that blipped in and out of focus as the train moved faster. He couldn't grasp this evil that she spoke of. He knew people were sometimes unfriendly, and also dangerous if they thought you had something they did not, but for the most part, no one other than the people who knew him best had ever hurt him. Even then, the pain was grounded in poverty and uncertainty, which came and went like bad weather. It was not an evil like what Brynja began to describe without his asking.

She offered examples of stories from far flung cities and towns that she had studied in school and in her legal training. The cases were crystallized in their horrible retellings. Though he knew these were the stories most suited to her explanation, he realized he didn't want them in his mind. He didn't want to know about the things people did to one another for reasons even they didn't comprehend or couldn't control.

As Brynja related the worst cases to Rilke of a world he had never known and had never had words for, he began to feel sick. Bodies turned up in odd places in all kinds of conditions. Animals and children who had been cruelly used. Investigators explored the minds of people who had done such things to others, and these case studies formed the basis for policies of deletion. Markers of aggression had been mapped near the turn of the century. If the patterns could be scanned and identified, and proven through interviews and tests, shouldn't they be wiped out of existence?

Rilke turned a sickly shade of green and within seconds, Brynja produced a bag from a sidewall drawer. She handed it to him just before he vomited into it.

"And that's the desired response." She passed him a tissue and he wiped his mouth and nose, still feeling queasy.

"When I relate stories like these to some individuals during advanced sessions, they do not get sick. Instead, they are aroused. Their brains light up with familiarity or recognition. Other protocols, until we are sure, and then our recommendations." She took the bag and the tissue from him and placed them in a nearby case. She pressed a button and then opened the case again. It was empty, and a half smile played across her mouth.

Rilke felt unwell and cradled his cheek with his hand as if his head was too heavy. He glanced out the window at the bright green landscape.

"Why are people like this at all?" He looked forlornly out the window.

Brynja fiddled with the edge of her sleeve. "There are several factors. Genetics, neural pathways, brain damage, abuse. These are all true."

She also began to look out the window, and also at her hands and her sleeve, as if it were the most interesting object in the train car. Fen rested, curled up in a cinnamon coil against Rilke's side. The fox had tired herself out and seemed to be resting deeply. Brynja was pleased to see the fox was recovering and smiled at Rilke briefly before continuing on with her history.

"Some claimed it was a virus. People hungered for excitement without consequence. Overpopulation, or maybe a mutation? Birthrates fell, life became more difficult. Preemptive editing was still controversial. But human society has required constant correction since the beginning. This is just the most advanced form." She finished her explanation and Rilke knew there was much more she was leaving out.

History had always fascinated him. He never learned enough at school, but when his uncle had talked, it was usually about the past.

"My uncle Afi said that slavery was like that. He said it was something that never went away, the desire to own someone else. He said that freedom was in the mind and slavery lived there also, but money and death were bigger than both of them. He said that is what caused the Collapse." Rilke felt the heat come into his cheeks but Brynja didn't seem to notice.

He could see her blush, however, when he said something she didn't know much about. She knew more than Rilke about much of the world, but little about the one he had come from, that he had inhabited since birth. He wondered if his ma and Afi would always be invisible, and the stadium too, unless he remembered them for Brynja.

Brynja was nice to him, and had helped Fen recover some from her ordeal but he saw how important it was for her to command, to be right, and to know. He wondered if she did that because she had to, not because she wanted to. And he wondered if she herself was enslaved in ways he could not grasp, just as he had been freer in the stadium in ways she could not grasp.

He was excited for the chance to help her understand. She wasn't the sort of person who would select only the things she wanted to believe in rather than the truth. He knew she had a knowledge of people, and also beings like Fen, who had been created for a purpose. That thought bothered him, but he decided Brynja had to know what his life had been like, so she could understand why it was important for him to travel north with Fen.

Brynja raised her eyebrows. "The Collapse?"

Rilke shifted in his seat, unsure if he had drifted in thought and she had to repeat herself or if she was asking for the first time. But there was anxiety too. No one had ever talked to him for this long and he was frightened. What if he didn't remember what Afi had actually said? What if he had said it wrong?

When he looked at Brynja he thought there must be more kinds of people in the world than he could ever imagine. And this too, this talking without worrying about hunting first, or being too tired to think about the stars and to tell stories sometimes, this was hard. People did so many things to stay alive, and sometimes it was through conflict and other times it was a tap of a finger to a brow and a line of speech.

And also this, to speak casually about the Collapse in comfort when there were people who had lived through it and lived as his extended family in the stadium. They could never have talked about it without singing walking songs, train songs, or boat songs. Someone might still be singing in a warm, lit corner about a journey to somewhere better that lay just ahead.

"The Collapse was just after the time when everyone drove cars."

Brynja nodded as if she knew what he meant, but other things about her face told him that he should keep talking, that there were still things she was curious about, that she truly didn't know or understand about what that time had been like.

"My ma's Oma had her very own car, but everyone had cars then. The gas was something you could buy. It was expensive, but everyone shared."

"You have a different perspective. We see the world from different angles, because we grew up in different places."

"How far are we from Savannah?"

"We are just a few hours by rail." She clarified. "It's just a way of thinking about distance. This is your first time on a train?"

"I've only seen them a few times, when I would sometimes walk north away from my home on a pretty night. I always wanted to know where everyone was going. I had only known the stadium." He found himself wishing to never return there, not even in his thoughts. But he probably never would. The whole family could wash away and he would never know. Would he want to know or would he always wonder?

"The stadium is where you lived?" Brynja asked with a heaviness and a slowness in her voice. It was as if someone took the bread he delivered and they seemed happy to see him, almost like they would invite you in though everyone knew that was not allowed. He had seen that look before, especially in older folks, though elders did not last long after a time. Occasionally the city came and took the elder somewhere else, especially when they weren't able to cook for themselves or stay clean.

Some people spoke of their going as if it were to a kind of heaven; a place where you could lie down and rest as much as you liked and didn't have to walk, hunt, or trade any more, and someone would feed you, and even clean you. He could see why someone like his ma would see that as a heaven. Others talked about it as if it were a living death. And others simply said that no one ever came back.

He thought about Old Sal and the woman with the cloudy eye and wondered if they still lived in the tattered blue house on the quiet street.

The Dining Car

Rilke had been obsessed with the idea of the dining car ever since Brynja had mentioned it. She had said she would buy him a meal before they reached Atlanta so he could save his credits. He had shyly nodded then. But the food Brynja had bought him earlier had just whetted his appetite. When she left to check on her new contracts, someone passed by the door of their compartment with a bag of delicious-smelling food. Something fried. Something hot. His stomach had growled. Now he was hungry again.

Much of the same scenery flashed by his window and Fen was sleeping again after all of the energetic play. He took the few credits he had left after leaving Savannah and shoved them in his pocket. Brynja had advised him to exchange the coins as soon as he could because city credits did not carry value too far outside their home area. Even though what he had wasn't much, he decided to transfer them to the currency she had suggested and test their buying power in the dining car. Brynja explained that the first class travelers were ahead of that car, even further on, so he figured there was no way he could get lost on the train.

"Here goes," he muttered to himself, as he stepped into the hallway.

The passenger car they occupied was many years older than the next one he encountered as he walked toward the engine. The corridor was similarly narrow, but instead of gray metal, it was dressed with a light wood and decorative light fixtures. It felt warm and homey. The cabins also seemed larger, but this was a guess. There were fewer doors than his own train car which meant more private space. Inside one he heard a loud snore that resonated from one end of the car to the other. He figured this must be a comfortable car to sleep in and moved along.

The next car was the same, and the one after that too, minus the snoring. In one car a family spoke a language he did not understand and had never heard before. In another, a woman laughed so hard she snorted like a pig, causing another woman to chastise her. "Now you mind your manners and sit up!" said the voice. All these people, thought Rilke. Going the same direction.

Though there were minor differences, like a door might show some scuffing or be a different color, each car was nearly identical to the other. His car seemed to be the oldest, simplest, but still a better way to travel than walking. He began to relax. It felt good to not worry about encountering other people who might hurt him or take his few credits. When he did see someone in a passageway, the interaction was limited and brief. Perhaps, "how do you do," or "excuse me," but nothing more. Everyone seemed lost in thought, only mildly present in the same place with him, but pleasant and at ease. He felt more at ease too.

Rilke had passed through more than one car and was beginning to wonder if he should have been counting as he passed through. Each carriage had its own character, with some trimmed ornately with designs he'd never seen before and others more plain and minimal. Some were finished in dark wood and others with some other hard material he didn't recognize. Some numbers on the doorplates were in silver and others were a deep gold or even brushed black metal.

In one he even saw a picture of a woman he recognized from an advertisement. She was smiling in the picture with her hands on her hips and a guitar was slung across her body. There were black marks on the bottom corner as if someone had written on it. When he recognized some of the letters of her name, his eyes widened. Had she been here, where he was standing? Had she signed the picture? He touched the name covered in thick glass. But there it was, signifying something.

He knew he was near the dining car when he smelled food and reached a car markedly different from the rest. Inside, the atmosphere was warm and convivial. It was brightly lit with several booths and one or two people occupied a few of the tables though it was not crowded.

The quiet clink of cups against saucers and murmur of conversation was a pleasing backdrop to the sizzling, frying sounds emerging from the tiny kitchen. Inside, a tall man with a turban worked quickly and confidently, as a small red-haired woman with a tidy apron whisked through the door which swung in and out each time she posted a ticket.

The diners were distributed through the car in quiet booths or at square tables, each lit with the glow of a single lamp. When Rilke entered the dining car he knew he wouldn't be able to afford the delights that had created the initial smells his nose had entertained. Still, he searched around the room until he saw the machine that Brynja had described.

"EXCHANGE CREDITS HERE," read the sign. There was a picture of a hand dropping coins into a funnel and other kinds of coin coming out. He approached the machine, hoping that it was as simple as placing his coins in and receiving state credits instead. It turned out that it was, but the end result was disappointing. He had dropped in all of his coins and received fewer back. Although he understood that the value was supposed to be equivalent, something about the new coins in his hand felt less real.

Was he really leaving everything he knew? Everyone he had ever met or talked with? His job with Kasim? Although his day-to-day life was spent working and reading a single book in his evenings alone, that was somehow enough. He had found all that he needed there in those pages. But meeting Fen had changed him, by giving him visions of things he desired, and this in turn altered everything else.

He took the coins and placed them inside a special pocket in his vest. The heaviness felt good, and somehow matched the solidity of his thoughts. He looked the machine up and down, marveling at the energy he felt after exchanging his coins. This was really happening. He was beginning his new life.

"Excuse me, are you finished?" A woman with heavy makeup and a scarf over her purple curly hair stood behind him, clutching a brown bag that appeared heavy with coins. He nodded and stepped aside.

He walked to a nearby booth and sat down as the menu projection glimmered before him. He could still see the woman using the exchange machine and was relieved when she dumped her city coins in all at once and received just a few coins back. Maybe all city coins were less valuable than state coins.

"What'll it be?" Another woman approached, wearing the black apron of a server. He had never ordered from a menu or sat in a restaurant, so all of this was new. He hesitated, then asked for more time. She moved to another table as he collected his thoughts.

What could he get with what he had in his vest? Should he take his money out now? What if someone came by and took his money while he counted it on the table? These thoughts made it difficult to concentrate. He looked at the menu and tried to make sense of it.

The least amount he could pay was for bread and the most costly dish was an expensive lab-grown roast that he had seen on a billboard during his furthest walks east from Kasim's. As hungry as he had felt before, he realized that he would have to make do with some Brunswick stew and bread. The uncertainty of the trip ahead was something he would have to contend with, but thinking about it now only made him anxious.

"Decided, hon?" The woman was back and she jotted his order down after bringing a glass of water. After she left, he looked around, trying not to appear out of place with his curiosity.

Directly to his right was a florid man and a plump woman with rosy cheeks. They had finished eating and were having an after-dinner coffee. They were sharing a piece of cake. He felt embarrassed by his desire and looked away.

At another table nearby, a bald, tattooed man with a long beard and mustache cut into the lab roast with a gusto Rilke understood. If that was in front of him, he would appear just as happy.

He could hear in the booth behind him two men arguing quietly about a trip they were traveling home from. Apparently one of the men had paid too much for something and his partner wasn't letting it go. From the conversation, Rilke could tell they shared finances and it hadn't been an easy trip. Something about the family estate and the trust.

Just then, his food arrived, and he tucked in, moving slowly and deliberately from enjoying the bread to dipping it in his soup and back again. It was good. Nearly as good as what his mother made in the stadium, but much richer. There was no gator meat in the stew; of that he was certain. He finished his meal and when the bill came, he timidly pushed forward the coin he thought would cover it and was relieved when it did. He was left with two small squares of metal, much lighter than the others. He would ask Brynja about them.

Rilke stood up, oriented himself once more, and walked in the direction of the tiny side kitchen.

Rilke was nearly through the dining car when he saw a nervous-looking middle-aged man seated by himself near the door. He was bent over a digital notebook similar to the ones Rilke remembered from school and also from the testers when they came to his classroom. The man looked official, even though his suit seemed slightly too baggy and he needed a shave. Rilke was walking past the man's table when he spoke.

"You, young person, come here for a moment, would you?"

Rilke came closer to the man and saw that he was indeed huddled over a notebook and that there were numbers in two columns.

"Can you read those numbers off to me? My eyes are a

little weak and my adaptive readers aren't working." The man wore thick chrome-rimmed glasses, and he briefly took them off. He tapped them twice on the side, and Rilke could see the distortions skittering across the lenses. The man put the glasses back on and scrunched his face as if showing Rilke how hard it was to see. Though he seemed comical at first, Rilke tried to be polite. Someone needed his help, and he liked helping.

Rilke held the notebook carefully so as not to damage it and began to read the numbers carefully aloud. When he reached the end, where he assumed the last number was the sum of all the numbers before it, he handed the notebook back to the man.

"Yes, yes indeed. Now what if I told you that you could make that much money and more if you invest just a little of your cold hard cash?"

"I'm . . . not interested, but thank you," Rilke had seen other people use this expression before whenever he approached them with the leftover rolls in his bag at the end of the day. Kasim always called it one of the benefits of the job. He said that if his workers chose to sell the leftover rolls, they would earn back a little to help them do their job better and more efficiently. And then if they ate the rations instead, he saw that in the same positive light. This was a way of keeping the morale high with his workers and also encouraging them to work harder for him. But Rilke often found that no one wanted to buy the bread at the bottom of his sack, so he gave it to the birds or ate it.

The man wasn't taking no for an answer.

"No wait, I need you to read that second column. It's my eyes, you see. I just get so tired and need a little help."

Rilke sighed and reached for the tablet again. It was the same as before except the numbers were higher. There was no sum at the bottom of the column, but when Rilke was close, the man said, "Press the red button on the right." As if on cue, a red button floated on the page next to the number. Rilke pressed it and the numbers exploded into glittery squares and rolled along as if on a string. He tried to turn away but wanted to see what they would do next. When the numbers stopped, they were on a much higher number than the previous column had been.

"Now tell me. Isn't that number higher? I bet it's at least in the 80s, eh?" Rilke nodded and briefly wondered how the man knew the amount since he hadn't been able to read the columns before. Then he realized the man was trying to get his interest in the numbers by having him read them.

"Look, I don't have money to invest in anything. I don't need anything. But thank you." Rilke tried to give the man his notebook back and walk away, but the man caught his attention yet again.

"I'm sorry kid, we got off on the wrong foot. My name is Sonny Vattencoy and I am in the business of selling hope and freedom. But when I'm not selling, I'm also buying. How about if I buy you a piece of pie since you were so kind to help an old man with failing eyesight? Would that be too much to ask? Listen to an old man talk about his life for a few minutes in exchange for a piece of pie?"

Rilke stood perplexed for a moment. Of course he wanted a piece of pie. In fact, he had forced himself to walk out of the dining car before he bought one. It would not keep him full but would only make him want more. He knew this but he had never had pecan pie and was wondering how it would taste, especially with whipped coconut cream. He had read the menu and saw the description and had read it to himself a few times before deciding he couldn't afford it. But here he was, wondering how to say "no" to free pie.

"I guess I could listen for a few minutes." Rilke looked at the empty chair, over at the kitchen where the pie would surely emerge from, and back at the man. Sonny Vattencoy wore a suit that was slightly too large, but he looked like he could afford the pie. He was relaxed and graying at the temples. He had already eaten by the looks of the plates beside him, so maybe he wanted some pie too. Maybe if he ate some pie, he wouldn't talk so much and it could be more like a regular conversation.

Rilke sat down in the chair and in just a minute the man had ordered an entire pie. The waitress placed it before the man who cut it into slices and placed the largest one on an empty plate. He placed it neatly in front of Rilke and then dolloped out the whipped cream which had also arrived at the table with the pie. Sonny slid the pie across the table toward Rilke and smiled benignly. Rilke began to take tiny bites so as to extend the joy that was exploding in his heart. Never had he tasted something so rich and sweet.

The man talked about numbers and interest rates as Rilke ate distractedly, focused on the pie and not so much on the man who droned on about insurance claims and certain parts of the state where risk was sold in quantities to guys like him who had a way of knowing how it was all going to turn out: the fishing season, the hurricane season, the season of this or that disaster that might destroy a small farm's crops, but they bought insurance and those companies would sell risk shares, where for just a little investment anyone could own a share of the risk and only be out that one small coin they invested. The benefit was over a long period of time so they could earn interest on their investment as well as on a fraction of the insurance payments that they could afford based on the multiplication of two factors . . . . and on and on he droned while Rilke ate the pie and marveled at how the nuts were firm in some ways and then buttery, smooth, and soft in others. The chef had the whip so pert and fresh with stiff peaks, Rilke understood it to be perfect without anyone telling him so.

"And all I would need would be your signature right here," the man said, as if Rilke had agreed to something, though he hadn't at all.

"What do you mean? I didn't say yes to anything." Rilke stopped tasting the pie and put the fork down.

"I said you could have a return on a small investment of let's say, oh, how much do you have in your vest pocket?" Rilke felt tricked in some way, but he wasn't sure how it all had happened. He was enjoying the pie and now the man was asking him to sign something and he knew exactly where Rilke's money was. How did he get to this point without noticing? Rilke's head began to throb.

"So how bout it, hmm? Timothy, was it? No? My memory is really bad. Now wait, it was Tony, right?"

Each time Rilke shook his head he began to wonder if the sweet treat on his plate was worth the unease he felt when the man started talking again. But what he felt was worse than unease.

"Look. This number here is the lowest I go for anyone. Surely this would be what you're looking for, right?"

Rilke blinked his eyes. If he looked, he was being drawn in again. If he said no, he might have to excuse himself and there would still be three bites of pie left on the plate, easily. He wasn't willing to leave just yet, but there was a danger here that he couldn't put his finger on. It made him uncomfortable and it made him question whether he was the first person the man had sought to lure into his scheme with a sticky, gooey dessert. He hadn't tasted the crust yet, but the moment his fork parsed the edge he knew it WAS worth it to listen to the man, so long as he was careful to not agree to anything. He felt a little flushed, like he was overheated.

"So, as we discussed, you would begin with a payment of around, oh, let's knock off 5% for your being a new customer. You're from Wadley, right? No, no, I think you said Jacksonville, no? Oh, my memory . . ." The man began to rifle around in his pockets like he was looking for something, then asked if Rilke had a pen. As Rilke shook his head, he noticed there were at least two bites more but they didn't look right. They seemed to shift.

"Oh, here it is. Now look." Sonny moved in close and leaned over the table like he had an important secret. Then, he took a notepad from his pocket that was made with a fine gold threading along the seam. The pages were a kind of vellum— that's the word he used—and he took out a tiny knife to cut the page from the notebook. As a flourish, he pulled a handsome golden pen out of his pocket and he scribbled something on the little slip of paper. It was a number. The man turned it over, and passed the paper across the table.

"There, That's my final offer."

Rilke looked down at the sheet of paper. He had no intention of buying anything at all, but he still picked it up and turned it over. He turned it back over and slid the paper back to the man.

"Thank you for the pie." Rilke struggled to put the fork down on the plate. He knew it was time to leave, even though there was more pie. The man was trying too hard to lure him into some kind of deal, and Rilke knew that the longer he stayed, the more risky it would become. The room tilted again.

"Okay, I can tell you are a discerning customer. This won't do, nope, let's see . . ." Sonny thumbed through a different little notebook and came to a list. Here he paused and glanced over at Rilke.

"You know, a kidney can go for almost two hundred in this market, and everyone is born with two. I can hook you up with a guy—"

Rilke pushed the chair back away from the table and stood up, perhaps too quickly. He put a hand down more forcefully than he'd intended, and his plate dipped against the table under the weight of his hand, flipping a scrap of pie onto the floor. This was the moment when he felt he should have gone faster than he did, but the room was spinning. He slumped back down into his seat. His throat tightened. Then it was hard to breathe.

There were two of the man, or possibly three, and then it was nothing but tablecloth until he closed his eyes. He heard Brynja's voice shouting across the dining car just as he blacked out. It could have been an allergy or it could have been a seizure, said a couple of people nearby. Later he would learn that Sonny had escaped unnoticed, and Brynja had been too occupied with reviving Rilke to track the man down.

Cases closing with a snap, cold against his forehead, the jab of a needle.

More shouting, then nothing but stillness.

When Rilke finally woke up, it was with the understanding that he had been out for a while.

"What happened?" He was lying across the seat and Fen was across from him flicking her ears forward and then to the side in nervous attention.

"You were unconscious. I was worried." She lay down and rested her head on her forepaws and looked up at him.

"I'm sorry. I shouldn't have left you alone like that. But I wanted to explore and I was hungry." He thought back to the pecan pie and how good it had tasted. Then, with a sinking heart, he realized the connection.

"There was a man. He was trying to sell me things. And then he said something about how much kidneys were worth. That was the last thing I remember." Both Rilke and Fen turned their heads as the door opened a bit and Brynja peeked in.

"You're awake." She came inside the compartment and had a cylinder in one hand, and a small bag in the other. "Here's coffee and a sandwich. I didn't know what you'd like so there's a couple of choices." Rilke looked at Brynja with gratitude and eagerly unwrapped his sandwich as she poured coffee from the steel cylinder into a mug.

"We'll be in Atlanta soon. There's already a mass of people on the outside of the train, so don't be too surprised." Rilke looked at her with a confused expression when she said this.

"Atlanta is a big city. Everyone hopes that they'll find work there, or maybe a way out of whatever mess they're in. So people who have been walking most of the way find ways to board without a ticket. They don't have a cabin or a place to sleep." Rilke nodded and sipped the coffee. It was good. He'd only had it a few times in his life. Sometimes there was coffee in the stadium. Kasim always had a pot brewing for his couriers and bakers in the morning. He said it would keep you alert.

"I'm sorry I wandered off like that."

"It's understandable. You were curious. But if you'd waited, I was going to buy you some food before I left the train. Now this sandwich will have to do." She smiled halfway, but gently. "There was something in the pie you ate."

Rilke nodded and bit into his sandwich. It tasted almost as good as the pie had, and he chewed each bite deliberately, pleased to taste a light chutney inside the bread. He couldn't remember if he had seen this on the menu. His head hurt whenever he tried to think too hard, so he focused on chewing.

"There was a man. At first I just thought he wanted me to give him money. He kept talking about investments and then he mentioned kidneys."

Brynja didn't look surprised. "Organs still have a market. Usually people who are trying to avoid hospitals look for other options. And they have money to pay extra, to pay people to find them as well as—you know where I'm going with this?" Given how sick Rilke had been before, she didn't want to turn his stomach yet again with some of the things she had seen and observed.

Rilke shivered. "I guess there was a catch to the free slice."

"Be careful about eating and drinking with people you don't know. People can justify nearly anything they do to survive. This is so purely human it cannot be excised from who we are."

Fen thought for a moment about what her own survival might require. She wasn't so different from Rilke or Brynja. But some of Canto's stories about foxes seemed ludicrous.

Though Rilke had known how to avoid danger when he was living in his tiny corner of Savannah, he did not yet know how to exist outside of that closed world. He had not realized there were people who would slip something in a drink or food in order to control them. He had not seen the man as a threat before, but in hindsight, Sonny had been motivated by money and nothing else. The free dessert was not a kindness, but an invitation to be tricked. Suddenly aware, and feeling revived by the food and coffee, Rilke checked his vest for his money.

"At least he didn't take my credits. I had just exchanged them."

"That's probably why he targeted you. He saw you turn in your coins. Then, when he realized you were alone, he made his move."

Rilke had finished the sandwich and was drinking his coffee, looking out the window. As the train took a turn, he saw what Brynja had described. All along the outside of the passenger cars there were people along the train, hanging from the sides. Then, he looked and saw another train, this one much smaller, local, with even more people perched on top of the train. They were so thick there wasn't room for even one more person. Kasim's coin had been worth more than Rilke could have imagined. Both he and Fen had been saved by Brynja's influence, and like it or not, he felt he owed her. This was a new feeling too. How many more things would he have to learn about the world before he was able to reunite Fen with Canto?

As they neared Atlanta, Brynja worried that Rilke would soon be without the protection that she provided. As assertive and business-like as she was most of the time, she had allowed herself to relax while spending time in the cabin with Rilke and Fen. Now she was preparing herself to reenter the world of work. She had already been checking up on her contract wards and preparing them for arrival in Atlanta. They would be bussed to a facility there before being assigned to their training sites.

From the preliminary scans she had done, only a few of the new workers required edits. A congenital hearing defect or an allergy was mild. There was one she had questions about though, which would require her to run some more tests in Atlanta. The deeper gene scans would reveal whether her initial evaluation had been accurate. It wasn't unusual to be given a false positive in the field and to have that diagnosis overturned in later tests.

She was mystified how violent traits continued to appear and reappear in populations that had been cleared before. Maybe the tests were just more sensitive now. Maybe the tests were not as comprehensively administered as they had been in the past. Whatever the cause, and as scientific as the process seemed, humans were irrational and their processes often were too. There was usually no explanation for why they did what they did or what lengths they would go to if they felt justified in doing so.

Brynja had long ago accepted the work she did as necessary. In college, she was more resistant, more inclined to argue against the conventional view. Once, when her ethics class debated a famous hypothetical problem, she had taken an unpopular position. On this particular day, the teacher had focused specifically on one particular figure from the twentieth century who had murdered millions of people and had convinced many others to do so as well. Some students in the class had argued that he should have been scanned in the womb and aborted. Others argued that he should have been deleted after he had started grade school, when testing would have confirmed his damaged core. Brynja's position was held by maybe only one other person in the class, and they never said anything during class, but only after.

"He should have been allowed to reach the age of twelve. Then, perhaps they could have sent him somewhere for editing." After Brynja had said this, she knew she had made a mistaken assumption about the real question the teacher had asked. Brynja was thinking about the conservative, practical side of the ethical problem. Humans might not act on the forces of their genetics. It was never for certain that he would have become the monster that he indeed became. At least she had believed that then, when she still had only seen the best sides of people, before her internship.

"Even though you could prevent the genocide of millions with the press of a button, you would allow the full resources of civilization to sustain this individual through childhood and into adolescence?" The teacher asked the question in that way that made Brynja's heart sink. Obviously, this was not the answer the teacher had wanted anyone to come to, at the same time he needed someone to walk into it, to be wrong, so he could be right. But Brynja was not going to let the teacher steer the argument so easily. She needed a perfect grade in this class so she could keep playing soccer.

"Yes. Because we do not know how much nurturing and treatment a genetically predisposed individual might need in order to be functional. Maybe his mother was mean to him. Maybe his father had brainwashed him." Here again, Brynja felt like her teacher was going to use her as an example of skewed thinking, and she was right.

"You have all of the evidence in your hands to indicate that this person has the potential to do what he did to millions of people, yet you are still building a treatment plan for him?" Professor Madox had a way of making everyone find humor in the most serious questions, a character trait that Brynja considered difficult to tolerate. Two or three students in the class snickered, and she felt angry. She imagined smacking one of the girls and that made her feel better somehow.

For one, her ancestor had been Jewish, and had barely made it out of Europe ahead of Hitler's invasion of Hungary.

She knew this history because she was taught to never forget it. Hearing someone snicker during a discussion about genocide was unacceptable. Brynja wondered if her college admissions had lowered their standards. It was a mean thought, but nearly everyone knew that someone who could think genocide was funny had a problem.

Brynja also had believed then that genetic behaviorism could have disastrous consequences if misused. She had taken this class to have that conversation. Who should determine editable or deletable traits? What is the line between voluntary and involuntary service if someone is desperate? Are they choosing? And how is that power not transforming society, by shaping what was heritable or inheritable, by removing the diversity of a genome hundreds of thousands of years in the making. The world was billions of years old. How could humanity, after nearly destroying the planet, still be the force to determine the future of its lifeforms in this way?

"Brynja. I think you are missing the obvious question that is hiding behind the question you are trying to answer now." Professor Madox came closer to her and leaned forward, placing his hand on the center table. "The question is not how should we treat this monster, but how soon and how thoroughly we can eliminate the potential for more like him. We need to think about our needs now as a society and what we want for the people of the future." Madox seemed sure of himself, and Brynja bristled at the way he used one part of the Haudenosaunee Constitution without considering sections that dealt with murderers by banishment.

"Professor, I just think you're using parts of a philosophy that's far bigger."

The teacher reddened a bit but then thumped his hand against the desk and did what he always did when he felt challenged. He asked everyone to take out their keypads and write their own response to the problem. He would let them write until the end of class then tell them to transmit their response to him before they left. But Brynja realized she didn't care. Not really. In fact, she had begun to tell herself that Professor Madox was right and the sooner she gave him the answer he wanted the sooner she could be done with this certification program and go to work. Then she could read all of the philosophy she wanted and make up her own mind about what the right choices were later.

What she didn't expect was his answer on her response, that she didn't see until long after the class was over. She had seen the grade was passing and decided that she must have told him what he wanted to hear. But that wasn't it at all. Instead, scrawled in his distinctive and nearly inscrutable script were three words. "I expected more."

After she had been out of college for a while, and perhaps already in her legal training the last year of grad school, she heard that he had walked out into the desert one afternoon and had never come back.

Overtime

In the third office hub of Building Two in the Atlanta Regional Scanning Complex, Janine looked at her nails and decided the sparkle wasn't bright enough. She'd need to adjust the program later anyway since it had begun to glitch. It said "moss" was green when she had looked it up. The codex had been wrong before, so she shrugged it off. One more glance in her compact, and she was about ready for her shift.

"Janine! You even listening? I said we had another FG67 case yesterday. You need to clean your ears, girl." Dee was shaking her head, and as she did so, her beehive bounced and her earrings flashed tiny messages. Janine thought the earrings were cool, but sometimes the things Dee said didn't match up with the messages, so Dee would be talking about something super serious and "Zowie Pop!" would flash for a second and then a small dancing frog would start a digital jig before appearing to hop into Dee's ear. It was disconcerting.

Janine moved her gum to the other side of her mouth and considered what Dee was saying. With her hair teased up stylishly on her head Dee looked just like that girl on *Yes to My Dreams* or at least Janine always thought so. Dee laughed it off every time Janine said this but blinked her eyes and tossed her head anyway.

Dee adjusted her seat and groaned when she had to stand up to reset the controls. She could never get that damn tilt right for her hip. After the accident, everything hurt. But she was at quota for drop-in doctor visits this month. Just three more days left of treatments and easily half a month of physical therapy more to go. At least it was free with this job.

Janine didn't even look at Dee, but went on regarding her nails. She didn't want her shift to start. She found her job of verifying sequences quite dull. Sometimes she imagined just pressing the button over and over again to see what happened. Probably no one would even notice. But she liked having a job, so she pretended to care. Besides, she was sure the higher-ups were checking everyone's work more often these days ever since the anomalies had become more frequent. Dee was still looking at her expectantly.

"What?" Janine was off in space most the time.

"I *said*, we had another FG67 yesterday."

"Two in one week? Must have been something in the water, huh?" Janine sighed.

The two of them had the dullest job. Both were lead dancers on the college channel show *Love Nights in Ur* and yet here they sat, pulling the graveyard shift. Gene scanning, instead of dancing for billionaires in Nome like they could be. Any idiot could do this job, Janine scoffed to herself. EASY. Just read the code and press the buttons and you're done.

Janine did begin to ponder Dee's point, though. Dee only talked to her about things that mattered, and Janine had begun to notice that if you listened to Dee, she seemed to know things before other people. Like she was one of those people who paid attention and remembered things. Janine could never get the hang of it.

Two in one week. The last time they had three consecutive pairs of FG67 cases in one month was when the Cortonsmith sextuplets had all been sequenced. It was big in the news. To think their numbers had been found in their division. What could you do? All them kids had to be expensive, right? It was practically a charitable act to call them up for editing, if that's even what it was really about. The whole family was moved uptown in one night. Maybe it wasn't bad at all, but like winning some kind of lottery. Maybe they were all geniuses or something.

Janine was either at work in this dump or up inside her own mind ever since Lou had called her back after a long hiatus. He was so creative. It was too much to think about at work so she forced the thought aside of Lou's face pressed against hers.

No, it wasn't a good time to think about that with Dee looking at her expectantly like Janine should give more of a damn than she did. And it wasn't even that she didn't like Dee, it's just that Janine had been working here longer and Dee got the same bonus everyone else had when they caught that GL32 that had gone unscanned until age twenty-one. Geez, you'd have thought the king was coming to town what with the parties and the board chairman bending over to praise the whole division and kiss Marcut's ass.

"Were you working?" asked Janine, turning to Dee, batting her extensions.

"Damn, Janine! When did you get those lashes?" Dee said it with real envy. She wasn't even trying to hold back.

Janine looked pleased. "Lou bought them for me after we

tried a new mode—you know, the one I was telling you about?" She giggled while Dee scowled, playing the prude against Janine's adventurous lifestyle. And yet she loved it, thought Janine.

Just then a light signaled the break was over and both scanners went back to their projection pods. The hum of the algorithm comforted Janine though she'd never admit it. Ever since worker resources had put in the new sensing mats she had learned to like the magnetic haptics of the data stream against her bare feet. The biometric input she offered assisted the AI in ways she still didn't understand. Fortunately no one expected her to. In fact, Lou's sister said they never called you back after the first interview if you knew too much, so Janine had played dumb. It wasn't hard at all.

Within seconds, the numbers began to parade across her zone and she allowed herself to drift back online. Easy-peasy.

When the third shift break was called, Janine stood up in the scan pod and stretched her arms. Dee was still rubbing her eyes and rolling her neck a bit, performing all the protocol adjustments they had learned in training. Each went to separate ends of the pod and danced to two state-approved songs, each gesturing "Good job!" and "High Five!" on the offbeats. Despite herself, Janine snickered and broke form while Dee closed the music session on the console.

"You looked so serious! Like you believed we were the high fliers of the week with the most editing recalls, I mean, like you believed this bullshit." Janine scoffed and worked to catch her breath. Damn. She just lost one of her lashes. Still, she clutched her belly which hurt from laughing.

Dee shrugged off the comment. "Why shouldn't I have a little fun? Maybe they're right. Doesn't hurt to move during the late Friday shifts."

Fridays were usually more backed up with requests and longer as a result, but no one complained about the extra pay. Overnight was the only way they made quota before Sunday dawn and it was only because of Janine and Dee that the whole place functioned at all. Everyone knew the scans had to be complete before weekend curfew or the city would be fined.

"I guess a little fun does make me work harder," mused Janine like it was a new thought. She tapped her knuckle on a tea cabinet and within seconds a dispenser opened and she took the cup, a nice northern variety, smooth and fruity. She always thought of Granddaddy when she drank sochi tea. He used to say their lives would have been different had he allowed the state to build that sand engine on his part of the beach. He held out for a better price and was pushed out. Had to sell cheap. But nothing would have stopped the tides, thought Janine. Certainly not a stupid sand drift deal.

"You ever think about them kids? The sextuplets?" Dee chewed on a toothpick absentmindedly. She recalled the morning she'd made the connection between the family in the news and the code she'd pinged two nights before.

"No. Do you?" Janine was already bored with the conversation and it hadn't even begun. What business was it of hers whether an FG67 or a GL32 meant anything? The algorithm flagged it, she approved it, and sent it along. Beyond that point was anyone's guess. Were they Einsteins? Rare anomalies? Or *sick in the digits*, as they used to say when she was little, and the adults spoke in whispers.

The only way anyone saw the connections was through extended family relations and neighbors. Gossip carried the names of people that were only numbers to Dee and Janine. It was better if it could stay that way, but sometimes stories stood out and then matched up with something they had scanned. Everyone said this job got to you after a while, but she didn't believe it.

Still, she remembered Tori and Windall, Samik and Frisby. Perhaps she shouldn't have allowed herself to go back that far, but she did, back to the kiss behind the school that she still kept secret. Windall wouldn't have been a genius, but maybe he'd been one of the other kind. Tori was smart, though. She was sure he went to some university somewhere to engineer algorithms or work logistics. Surely he wouldn't have been refitted for the ships. Not him, but maybe Frisby. She remembered watching Frisby harass the one dog in the neighborhood until it finally kept walking out of town and never came back. If anyone required an edit, it was him.

At this point, Janine realized Dee was still talking, and pulled herself forcibly back from the abyss of wondering what had happened to Samik. She was the one that Janine thought about the most. Images of Samik flashed back to Janine and she felt an anticipation that surprised her. It was just as before, and she remembered the feel of Samik's hands and lips on her face in a game that was never repeated. Janine drank her tea and Dee talked, but it didn't really matter any more because soon the tea was gone and the break ended like the others and the numbers went across her screen signaling time was up.

There was a moment when Janine almost drifted into something like sleep, but then there was a click in the back of the pod which signaled the arrival of a supervisor. So Janine feigned wide-eyed attention and went on following the numbers as they streamed across her console. The haptics would let her know if there was something she needed to approve. Always needed a human to seal the deal. International law required it.

Janine could feel someone looking over her shoulder, but she let the feeling go, concentrating on her work until she felt the figure move away toward Dee's console. There were some quiet words then Janine heard Dee get up from her seat and leave. It was almost time for break when Dee returned, and Janine could barely contain her curiosity.

"Who was that? You in trouble?"

Dee shook her head. "Nah, they just needed my help with something."

"Your help?" Janine tried not to let her question show through too plainly. She had been here longer than Dee and it didn't make sense that they would ask her for help first. Now she was invested in knowing the details. "You didn't answer my question."

"Yes I did. I'm not in trouble." Dee turned off the alarm of her console and stood up.

"Well, who was that?" Janine repeated. She could tell that Dee was being evasive. She turned off her own console and stepped toward the break area.

"Just one of the bosses. They needed a scan." Dee knocked on her soda cabinet and it dispensed a pink fluid that fizzed and smelled like cotton candy.

"I don't even see how you drink that stuff." Janine could tell that Dee wasn't going to budge. She also knew for sure now that she wasn't supposed to know. Dee wasn't giving any clues about who or what. That meant it was secret. Eventually they would be out clubbing and Dee would spill everything. Or maybe she won't, Janine thought again. Either way, she knew that Dee had done an extra scan that she couldn't talk about. And sometimes, that's all anyone ever needed to know.

Siena

Siena adjusted the visor as she settled into the seat, working her long black mane into a single braid. It was another blistering October in northern Georgia. She didn't mind the heat but she often worried about the unyielding sun and its effect on the farm she had worked so hard to build. It ate at her sometimes, how it could be so hot, drought-like, then be dumping buckets from the sky. It had always been this way, but lately it was getting to her. Just when the weather seemed to be settling in some places.

Siena knew she was not an easy woman to live with. Florence had said so this morning when trying to divert her back to their conversation after breakfast. There had been a message from Sangreave saying that there was a walker down at the station in Gainesville. After ten years? Flummoxed as Siena was, she was also ecstatic. Maybe there were still people out there who believed in the dream. But Florence thought otherwise, or at least it seemed so at certain times.

"You're saying you still want to be on call to drive people around and let them camp in our yard? When we can put all this behind us and focus on the farm?"

Florence had expelled this last bit in a huff. Florence thought it was time for Siena to officially retire from the bureau, sell the truck, and start taking her check. Their last fuel bill still lay on the table, sheer extortion from Florence's perspective. Siena reminded her that the money from selling the lemons this year easily covered the cost, just before slamming the door and walking out.

As Siena threw the truck into reverse, she tapped the brakes. She hadn't been sure if the fix would work. This truck meant something to her, and to the people who had once piled into the back making room for the others. For those travelers, walking had been their only option, so they were grateful for the truck to the trailhead. Siena still sometimes received letters from people who had made it to the end.

They had begun with nothing but had found everything on the Narrow Road. At the end they found connections. They found it in the people they encountered along the way. They found it in themselves. Siena never tired of helping people get started, or even delaying them if she didn't think they should travel. She always had work for them on the farm and she had learned long ago that people could still surprise her.

The truck rocked side to side down the hollow's rocky lane. She needed to get Sangreave to grade this for her, she thought for the second time this week. The truck glided out from the dark lane into the hazy filtered sunlight of the main road which was lined with oak and maple. Siena had been a part of this forest's recovery, indirectly.

As a young girl in Tennessee, she had helped her

Momaw Willie manage a tree nursery there that had started many of the giant timber further south, before the quake. The crisis had once been that there weren't enough trees. Now, if anything, the forests thrived and the agricultural landscape took a slower but sure path to recovery and balance. People were still adapting to a generation of smaller farms, of growing their own food, thanks to the permaculture movements of the previous century.

None of it had come quickly enough and further out there were other kinds of problems. Infrastructure had regressed and there had been decades of people passing through. So many countries had fallen since the late twenty-first century and even now with famine and drought or viral illness defining harder boundaries, she saw no future to the west, east, or south. That was *her* perspective, as Florence would say. Maybe other people could make such a life work even if she didn't know how. But she feared the shape of what would force so many people into the unknown. Siena had always wanted to build something solid and sustainable and letting go or moving on didn't fit into that vision.

The truck was a relic of this stubbornness, on its third or fourth engine using reclaimed fuels. It spoke of a nostalgic past but was familiar to newcomers. If she had pulled up to the reception office in anything but this old truck, people wouldn't have recognized the path away from the world they were leaving behind. Whether life in a glittering harbor was better than what could be had on a mountain farm, who was to say? She'd take the latter along with the inconvenience that such a life provided.

Siena draped her work-toned arm out the window and waved the bus around her. The silvery titan whisked swiftly past her and she could only guess what labor agency had put such a monstrosity in this part of the world. Increasingly, folks were either settled down like she was with a self-sustaining farm and a community of like-minded individuals or they were choosing to move where the work was, so long as that work didn't involve digging, heat, or harvesting. Never mind how hard life could be in the shipyards or in the bellies and backsides of cities.

The bus faded out of view until it was just a flash of light headed around the curve. On the downhill stretch she shifted into second gear and coasted. Briefly she tapped the brakes as another bus passed her a little too fast for the curve. The navigation system must have managed it just right because the bus was already around the curve and up the next hill as she started into the turn.

Resting her arm against the warm metal, she enjoyed the evening breeze against her face. She wondered who was waiting at the station. A family of five? Perhaps a young couple given the token as a wedding gift? No honeymoon I'd want, thought Siena. More like a half year trek and easily one of the harder ways to get north. And that's why she stood by her dream.

If you made it all the way with the same group of people, that was a sign. If you were the only one out of four, then that meant it was your time to make the trip, but not theirs. Whatever the case, the Earth would help you figure it out. Walking the Narrow Road would give you plenty of time to think about it.

Siena arrived at the station's receiving area and took a vendor's ticket on her way into the complex. At least some things haven't changed, she thought. She made her way to the checkpoint and flashed an identification chip at the clerk who paused for a moment before scanning it.

"Don't see too many of these anymore."

Siena considered how different she must look from the woman on the attendant's monitor. Then, she had been in the best health of her life. Now, with the arthritis and ten more years of life behind her, she was surely a different Siena Greatwood to most observers. Still tall, full-bodied with broad shoulders. Black hair past her waist, now more silver than before. But still wild, a bit like her eyes, shadowed by thick eyebrows that seemed knit in scrutiny. In the picture that the oh-so-young clerk studied, her lips were probably fuller, maybe even smiling. Her chin more pronounced, a clearer line to her neck. She was still that fierce woman, just a little more mellow. Maybe the clerk saw this too because she reluctantly handed the chip back to Siena.

"You should get this updated, Dr. Greatwood."

Siena rolled her eyes and took the chip back. "Thanks, Tish. I'll do that."

The clerk was getting ready to say her name wasn't "Tish" but Siena was already striding into the facility with the confidence of someone who had done this many times before, and for longer than most of the employees had been there. Perhaps with the exception of one person.

"Doll!" At Siena's commanding shout, a tall figure with graying dreads past his knees looked out from the booth. Angular frame, graceful movements. Siena was grateful to see Doll had not changed.

"Well, I'll be damned. Siena Greatwood!" Doll broke into a smile and emerged from the booth with arms wide. Even as tall and as broad as Siena was, Doll folded her in his arms and squeezed her until she thought she would snap.

"Where have you been? For ten years, no less?" Doll's arms were crossed and his voice chided gently.

Siena gave a sideways smile and shrugged.

"I've just been on the farm, you know. Florence keeps me

busy." She fussed with a pen in her overalls and, satisfied that it was in order, glanced up at Doll's face. He had just one wrinkle or two, though it would take a friend to see it. Same open expression with delight playing along the edges, deep brown eyes, arched brows.

"Seriously. What kept you away?" Doll inclined his head, curious,

Siena shrugged. "I guess there aren't as many tokens left. Not nearly as many people choosing to walk these days. I was passed by two FVs on the way here. Looks like the contractors are doing well enough."

Doll nodded. "About every kid on my street is either headed for college or the shipyards, I've been seeing more lonely parents at the group dinner. Everybody is middle-aged around here."

This last part struck Siena as funny. "Welcome to my world, Doll."

Doll's quiet, almond eyes always seemed so exotic to Siena, especially when lined with intricate patterns as they were now. Remembering he had asked her a question, Siena inhaled and let her breath out once before responding.

"I just miss the days when I was headed to Dawsonville twice a day, helping to process walkers needing a ride to the trailhead. They saw the dream the same way I did, as a place you found with your feet. As a place that was on the other side of a lot of thinking. Things only the Earth and the mountains can provide or help you work out."

Doll could see it on her face, a sadness that seemed like deflation. Siena appeared more tired than he remembered. Tired from talking, tired from being friendly.

"The train just arrived, and I think this passenger came from Savannah. Sangreave said he wasn't taking people up to Dawsonville anymore, so I didn't expect you to make the trip.

Still driving that dinosaur?" Doll wasn't surprised when Siena ignored the question.

"Just one?" Siena was perplexed and a little let down. Normally a token brought more than one person, whole families, extended relations. That had been the aim of the census takers. Gainesville would process the walkers, record the names of those who passed through, and this data would be, for some people, the only record they had ever passed through Georgia. Some people came from places as far away as Costa Rica, though over the course of a generation or two. Had people in the last century known how hard things would become, they would have begun the migration then. But it never surprised Siena when people denied the reality of what was all around them.

"One walker, huh? Let's see who they are."

With that, Siena and Doll headed toward the station's interior.

Doll and Siena were both surprised when they realized the single passenger was not merely alone, but a youth. The only problem with the census was that people often came from places bearing no identifying information whatsoever. No passports, no chips, not even anything that pretended to be a record of where they were from. The state had been so satisfied with the endpoint documentation data they gathered through the Narrow Road Project that they let slide other questions like how old people were or whether they were even related. So stark were some of the conditions people lived under, the only meaningful data was what could be collected in Maine.

Stations along the Narrow Road also helped, but overall the vast majority of walkers were beginning a life so new their previous existence mattered little. Besides, there was additional processing after the Narrow Road, and that often included biometric reviews. No individual avoided intake upon arriving in Maine. And from what anyone could make of it, Maine's data was the only part that mattered to countries as wealthy as Canada when determining entry.

The kid was thin, and clearly someone used to living in a city. They bore no evidence of having walked and camped their way up from Florida or Texas. People accustomed to migratory life had a solidity about them that reassured Siena. They would make the trek just fine. But again, she had been surprised before.

"Hey there." Siena took in the look of the youth: lean, long face, dark eyes with long lashes, curly hair. An unmistakable gentleness, innocence too, but also a weariness. But an excited and curious expression crept up from a mouth which rapidly opened into a shy, but genuine smile.

"Hi." The kid extended a hand as if to shake and Siena noted the hiking duffel that leaned along the bench. All of the youth's possessions. "Oh!" The kid quickly reached into a pocket and pulled out a faded color brochure about the Narrow Road. "I'm looking for Siena Greatwood. She's supposed to help."

Siena regarded the brochure quizzically. She hadn't seen one of these in almost a decade. She didn't realize they still existed, but apparently the kid had one which meant there were still people out there who knew how this worked. She took the brochure and shook the kid's extended hand. It was warm and dry, unlike what she expected. The kid was bashful, but not nervous, so it was unlikely that they were evading the law or hiding anything.

"Call me Siena. And you are?" Her eyebrows raised kindly and she smiled again.

"I'm Rilke."

Siena liked how pleased the kid seemed by everything. She wondered to herself, who could be that happy? But she was always delighted to see people still had a sense of humor, knew how to treat strangers kindly, and were willing to attempt such a long trip.

Her concerns minimal, she adopted a relaxed stance and began walking to Doll's office. "Come with us, Rilke. We need to ask a few questions and then I'll take you to the farm." At this, the kid's eyes grew large.

"But . . . I'm only nineteen. I'm strong. I can work!"

Realizing what the kid thought she meant, Siena and Doll shook their heads at the same time and laughed. Doll leaned forward a bit to make himself less imposing.

"No, honey, we're not talking about *that* farm. Siena has a home place not far from here and she helps travelers get ready for the long walk."

Doll's explanation must have been satisfactory because the kid seemed reassured. Doll made a mental note to speak more slowly and explain the process more fully. It had been a long time since he had needed to relay the workings of what had once been a successful interstate program.

"We're just taking your information so that we can enter you into the system and pass it along. People will be watching out for you in case you run into trouble or need to get a message to someone back home." Rilke nodded to show he understood. Doll's soft voice was always comforting, thought Siena.

Nineteen? Siena speculated that Rilke could be anywhere between twelve and twenty-five. Sometimes people were far wiser than their age and sometimes the opposite. But this kid appeared to have all that was required to make a positive first impression. It was promising. She often told people that she could tell the character of someone within one minute of meeting them. In all of her years, she had rarely been wrong. And this kid, whoever they might be, seemed alright to her.

Processing complete, Rilke and Siena made their way toward the parking lot. As expected, there was a lack of documentation, but there would be plenty at the end of it. A clean start, as long as his genetic scans were clear. Siena disliked the end of the process, but understood that it was the price of citizenship. Most people were willing to pay any price to leave where they had been before.

They walked down an old hallway that still smelled the same as she remembered it. Somehow the train station's hallway smelled just like her elementary school. Must have used the same cleaner. She looked over at Rilke as they walked. The bag was almost half as tall as Rilke, but looked full and empty at the same time. Not like a regular pack that was stuffed with a sleeping bag and clothes.

When Rilke handled the bag like it was a child, Siena noticed. She had seen this kind of carefulness before, usually when families would bring a beloved dog, cat, or even a chicken. Once, she had seen a monkey, perched on the shoulder of a particularly sneaky-faced child of six. She was sure those two created a great deal of mischief when they were on the trail.

But yes, she saw it. The precious way he rested his hand on the bag as if to reassure himself it was there. The almost imperceptible energy that she felt coming from the bag, as if it were alive or listening.

"My truck is this way." Siena held the heavy door open and waited for the kid to walk through. Hesitant, Rilke squeezed the bag close to his chest before stepping out into the hot night air. He was not usually out at night, not in his home city, and here he felt that same empty and forbidding darkness that he knew back home.

Sensing Rilke's hesitancy, Siena stopped wondering about the bag and reminded herself she had a job to do. People were generally tired after a trip like his and she assumed he had not slept much. It was time to act like a human and go with her gut. This kid had nothing to hide, and if it were a little dog or a cat, who cared? She felt a pang in her chest, and reached up to adjust her overalls and make sure her pen was in its pocket.

"We are parked right over there." Rilke looked where she gestured, about twenty yards away under a solar lamp.

"We're riding in that?"

Siena's first response was to defend her truck, but then she saw the kid's eyes. Even in the dim light of the streetlight, Rilke's expression was filled with awe and adoration. That look was what she always hoped for. Somehow this old Ford inspired people to think about how far they had come and how some technologies persisted into the long obsolescence of myth and dream. When this truck had been created, trains were considered archaic, even romantic, but to think that now seemed laughable. And yet it was true. Florence had verified it for Siena in her copy of *The History of the American States, Vol 5.*

Siena opened the truck's door which gave a raucous but satisfying metallic squeal. The kid leaped in before she could offer to take his bag. She had wanted to know what was in there before they got on the road for a winding hour-long ride back to the farm. But there was no easy way to ask and she needed to let it go for now.

"You good? You know how this works?" She held up the seatbelt and he nodded.

"In the stadium there was a seat I liked and it had a belt on it just like this."

His belt clicked into its casing and he grinned. A witness to so much displacement, but still capable of wonder. Siena caught herself again, imagining a terrifying early life for him because it was terrifying for her. She tried to imagine a world where nothing was the way she would choose, but was normal and natural for others. A place she could not control, manage, or engineer. At this, she shuddered, and tried to feign cheerfulness for the kid's sake.

"Have you ever ridden in a truck before?"

Rilke shook his head.

"After the Collapse, no one in my family had a car. No one that they knew had a car either. We all had parts of cars which we sold when we needed credits. But only rich people had cars and not anything like this."

Siena knew what he meant. She had seen vehicles that defied the imagination. Some hovered, some went really fast, and most were self-navigated, though they were restricted to certain classes of highway. Gas burners like hers were as rare as hens' teeth. Most people found the steel more valuable and chose to forgo the problem of finding fuel and purchasing it. No one without a permit could buy it, and not without a good reason. She was almost at the edge of not having a good reason, but having a farm and maintaining a forest for the state had its benefits.

The buses that had passed her on the way to the station were a new exception. Offshore recruiters from Iceland, Greenland, and Norway weren't unusual here, but Chinese companies were also beginning to explore the labor market here. Their contracts were often competitive too, sometimes offering a pension after fifteen years of service as opposed to twenty, but everyone knew that there were easier jobs than shipping.

Scrap haulers, pickers, and fuel finders could make it

well enough freelance, as could mechanical engineers, in this part of the country. There would always be jobs for folks who could make, remake, and unmake materials by hand. Too much had been overtaken by machines, even though it did make life easier for a lot of people. Depended on where you lived, for sure.

After all that she had heard, she would rather be a picker or a planter than a shipper any day of the week. And truthfully, avoiding interactions with contractors was how she had lived her life for the past thirty years. She didn't trust biometric shapers or geneticists and she didn't like any kind of artificial intelligences either. Too many people had been dealt a wrong hand because of an algorithm, or bad code, either by birth or under the scrutiny of legal statisticians. Some processes were not to be trusted, even with human oversight, because humans were not predictable. She had seen people change beyond what anyone would have thought possible. And just because a human sat at the end of a process didn't make it any less automated.

Siena climbed in on the driver's side and rolled down the window. She wanted to hear the engine when she turned the ignition. The heat was stifling, even in the darkness, and the cabin had become unbearable while she was in the station.

"This is what they call a three on the tree. You shift using this lever here." Siena touched the gear shift on the steering column with her hand lightly. She applied the brake and turned the key, pleased when the truck started without effort. She looked over at Rilke who brimmed with excitement.

With a bit of a lurch, the truck moved into gear as they headed for the gate and Siena fished out her chip. Soon they were rolling out of Gainesville through empty streets, which gradually gave way to moonlit swaths of highway rimmed with trees.

When they arrived at the farm, the air had cooled off considerably, especially as the night breezes threaded deeper through the mountain's forest. Siena was reminded of her childhood in East Tennessee, when her grandmother allowed her to run wild, dressed only in a makeshift loincloth. The Cherokee had once lived in those hills, and other people a thousand years before.

Getting by had been hard for so many decades, even during her grandmother's youth when the migrations first began. Siena thought it a paradox worth solving: to recover the land at the same time it was a means for others to pass through it. She even did the unthinkable by leaving for Georgia. Along the way she passed steady streams of camper caravans headed the opposite direction.

The story that Rilke had told her about his life in the stadium aligned with what she already knew about the cities just south of her. But then, he also seemed remarkably stable for a kid who had lived without the assurances she had always known.

Rilke quickly undid the seatbelt and hopped out of the truck before Siena could help. As she came around to his side she saw that he held the large bag even more closely to his chest.

That's an awfully good dog, she thought to herself. Determined to get the truth out in the open, Siena broached the subject.

"What's in the bag, Rilke? I have a right to know."

At the station, Doll had asked this in a roundabout, official-sounding way, but with no satisfying answer. Siena wondered if Rilke had understood the question. But here, on her own farm, Siena could be specific.

Rilke cast his eyes down and even in the near dark, Siena

could tell that he struggled.

"Please. She's my friend."

Siena motioned toward a table along the covered sidewalk that approached the house. There was a strong light there that she flipped on as Rilke gingerly set the bag down. But before either had a chance to say another word, the bag exploded into a reflective darkness as the form fled past Siena into the blurry dusk of the night.

"What the hell!" exclaimed Siena in a surprised shout that made Rilke jump even more than he had at the flurry of motion that was Fen.

"She's sort of a fox, but—"

"What do you mean, bringing it here?" As difficult as it was to ruffle Siena, this encounter had done so. Nothing had ever moved so fast that she could not identify it. Whatever had been in that bag flew with the certainty of a creature keenly aware of its surrounding, even from inside a bag.

Rilke looked down, and defeated, reached into his satchel. As he held the envelope out to her, she noted it had been his last resort to share this information with her. His intentions had been to conceal what was in the bag, from Doll, from her, from everyone. The realization infuriated her. She hated deceit, especially in those she was trying to help.

She snatched the envelope and opened the flap while angrily eying Rilke. Meanwhile, three beetles and a light-drunk hornet began to circle the lamp above them. She pulled out the letter and grimaced when she also had to pull her specs out of a pocket near her pen and put them on to read. She had managed until now to do without them, but this was not a moment for pretending she could read what was printed in the hazy light.

The letter contained information about the wildlife unit that Rilke was accompanying north to reunite with its owner.

It was written by someone granted federal rights to headhunt in the South. What's more, the letter indicated, Rilke was expected at the processing station on the other end of the Narrow Road with a temporary authorization expiring in one year. The rest was encoded for the processors at the other end of the trail and judging from the quality of the digital paper and the chip codes in the bottom corner, this recruiter had an interest in Rilke completing the trip.

"You are already in a contract? Why did the recruiter not take you north by rail?" Siena tried to control her tone as she said this to Rilke, but his dishonesty against the backdrop of her life here—the farm, her work with the census—was a little too much. The fact that it was a remote intelligence unit in his bag made Siena chew her bottom lip in a fury she could no longer hide. What government's equipment was running loose on her farm and to what purpose?

Rilke continued to look down, frightened, but aware this was his one chance to get everything right.

"Fen is special. I found her when she was sick. The person who gave me this letter helped us when we were on the train, and said that if I showed this to anyone who had questions, they would help."

Siena folded the letter and placed it back in the envelope. She shook her head, still in disbelief.

"Look here. I'm just disappointed that you lied to Doll and hid all of this from us. We are trying to help you, but we have to trust you." Siena sounded hurt and her hair stood out from around her face where it came loose from her braid. It made her appear more fierce in the light, especially coupled with the loud buzz of the hornet. Rilke was trembling a little.

Despite his fear, Rilke looked directly at her, resolved.

"I did not lie. I said I wasn't employed, and that I wasn't transporting an animal or property belonging to any government or corporation. She's only wanting to get home."

As he finished speaking, a face appeared from the edge of the patio. The rest of Fen's body emerged in the dim light as she allowed herself to become visible. The chromatophores in her fur displayed the cinnamon coat of a fox with black, triangular ears, and her eyes narrowed in a catlike grimace.

"What Rilke says is true," said the fox, in a tone that rang clearly in Siena's mind.

The thought appeared unbidden. This was not a familiar interaction, nor one that Siena had ever wanted. But unmistakably, it was a message meant for her, as the fox crept forward, low to the ground. Fen settled a few feet from Siena and placed her snout on her paws. Her large ears were flat against her head and her amber eyes blinked slowly, twice. In a way, the fox even looked a bit like Webb did whenever he knew he was in trouble.

"I can work for you. Don't fault Rilke." Fen's eyes and her earnest insistence pushed against Siena's anger.

Florence appeared by Siena then, having taken in the scene from the steps of the house. She had heard the commotion and had come outside without anyone noticing. She touched Siena's arm gently.

"Baby, there was a call from the station. Someone wanted to make sure that these two had arrived safely. You might want to call them back." Her calm voice defused the tension and Siena looked down at the petite woman beside her whose life and love meant so much to her.

"It's an AI." Siena said this with a solemn voice, as if she were fighting to accept the truth of it. Florence nodded and took Siena's hand.

"You've been needing to get a view on the orchard. Perhaps this unit can help."

"Her name is Fen," Rilke added hopefully, "and we can

both work to pay you back."

Siena had already decided the boy was not ready to make the trip, even with his high quality pack and rogue wildlife unit. The season was far too late for a trip through the mountains. Even in October it could snow at the higher altitudes, or worse. The sky could lay down an ice storm that would kill an unprepared trekker at over five-thousand-foot elevation. Rilke had no money, his shoes would not do, and his naïveté had already cost him her trust. But there was something genuine, and an empathy that reassured her. He had left everything behind to offer aid to something that wasn't even real from her perspective.

Siena shifted her weight to the other foot and forced herself to think practically. There was the cavern on her property that she had yet to explore as well as a borer beetle infestation she was trying to define the edges of. There were also areas on her property impossible to reach, partly due to her age and size, but mostly because she was terrified of rattlesnakes. If she could get the fox to perform a wildlife assessment, Siena would be ahead by months of work.

While Siena was thinking these thoughts, Fen stared intensely at the hornet, still circling the light above them. The fox stared at the light, which split in two for a second in a pulse then gleamed brighter. Then the insects attracted to the light all simultaneously moved away from it and back into the night. After they were gone, Fen looked at Siena in a way that she considered smug. Could foxes be smug? It certainly appeared to her they could.

"I can help in a lot of ways you haven't thought of." Fen projected.

Siena had heard of wildlife units capable of emitting high frequencies for different purposes, and this must have been a demonstration. Great, mused Siena to herself. An expensive insect repellent in the shape of a mammal. At this, Fen made a chittering sound like a sneeze, which Siena could not help but hear as laughter. Did the fox have a sense of humor? Did the fox hear her thoughts?

"You hungry, sugarfoot?" Florence pulled her braids along her left shoulder and wrapped her right arm around a relieved but visibly exhausted Rilke. She beamed at him and this made up for the missing courage that had already abandoned him before Fen sent the hornet away. Rilke was eased by the question and recognized some of what he was feeling as hunger.

"I have collards and smoked lab ham on the stove. I bet you haven't eaten in a while." Florence smiled at Rilke again and he felt like he did when he was still a small child. His ma had been tender once or twice, especially after he had been sick.

"No ma'am, I haven't. Thank you." Rilke relaxed, and Florence appeared pleased, except when she looked at Siena. Daggers were flying at her, but Siena took them as justified, crow-eating penance for her behavior.

The kid was shy again, Siena noticed, and she felt remorseful for having shouted at him. She was sure that was not the first time someone had done so, and she didn't mean to revisit that time in his life. It was not like her to be her most intimidating self. Why had she been so angry?

Rilke grabbed his bag back from the table and moved closer to Florence. He looked at Fen and then back to Florence. "Can Fen come inside with us? She says there's a black bear about thirty yards out past the truck and it might be wise to go in for the night."

Siena's jaw dropped. So there *was* a bear raiding her pawpaw patch.

"Ask Siena and see what she thinks," Florence smiled

encouragingly at Rilke and glared at Siena, who eyed Rilke with resignation.

Rilke looked back at her and she saw all of it again, the kindness, the wonder. When had she become so mistrustful? Florence was accepting Rilke openly, and it was clear that where Rilke went, the fox would go too.

"Nah, babe, it's alright." Siena spoke first to Florence and then to the kid and Fen. "You're both welcome." Siena looked down at Fen who continued to lie still, appearing to shift from red to silver and back again. Siena sighed. She couldn't believe she was going to apologize to a machine, but then it felt right. She also knew Florence expected it.

The Farm

Siena and Florence lived in a house that had been built in layers, one alternative building technology over the other. Florence had a lot of words to describe the styles, but Siena patted her arm gently twice as if to say, "It's been a long day." The four of them made their way toward a door framed with flowers and small trees at the end of the walkway awning.

In the 1930s, someone had cleared a scrap of land and built a spring box. There may have been a log cabin at that point but there was no way to be sure. In the mid-twentieth century, someone had bricked in a large hearth and had installed the cast iron stove that still roared some winter evenings when guests came to revisit the lodge.

Twenty years after the hearth in the timber-framed lodge was built, an Earthship backed against the wall of the hillside and wrapped around like a long hallway. Its tall windows took in passive solar heating. Here and there, signs of recycled wine bottles and timbers were locked in with cob, and sometimes brick or stone. In other places, old window panes or car doors were recycled into ports where one could look out on the mountains. "When it's not dark," Florence added.

Along the walk through this hallway, Florence directed Rilke to open a small door. He opened the door revealing a patch of straw. Florence said this proved that straw bales were behind the wall. In some places the wall was ten feet high. In other places the window sills and walls were beautifully shaped with tiny alcoves. In these alcoves, figurines of women or cats curled into circles. In another place, a long-limbed gazelle reached her head down to drink from an invisible lake.

"From your brow climb leaf and lyre." Lines from the poet emerged from Rilke effortlessly. Florence looked back in amazement and delight. Rilke added, "That's from the poet, Rilke. It was in a poem about a gazelle."

Florence smiled and patted his arm. "You like to read! Then we have much to talk about."

Rilke continued to stare at the statue.

"You like that?" Florence asked. He nodded.

She picked up the stone gazelle and placed it in his hands.

"Feel that good earth, honey? That's what holds us to who we are, through our roots." Rilke noticed they were almost eye level, but then Florence also seemed a bit shorter. Siena was nearly two heads taller, a giant compared to the small, gentle Florence. But when Florence stood up on the balls of her feet and then danced down, he could tell that she expressed herself through motion as much as through words. In this way she was much taller and more alive than any of them.

Siena was different. She seemed to Rilke to be like wood and fire all at once. Someone who could be warm and encouraging, but also unyielding if she needed to be, like a tree trunk. He knew she was a good person though, because everything she said or did was for the sake of Florence. And though to an outside observer it might look like Florence was the smaller of the two by virtue of her height, the reverse was true. Siena was firm and somewhat grumpy-seeming, but softened by Florence's chastisement. It was a dynamic he marveled at the more he observed it. He relaxed more with each minute he spent in their home and with the two of them, feeling their welcome.

He carefully touched one of the antlers of the gazelle and marveled at how smooth its lithe body was, how miniature its hooves. He offered it back to Florence, grateful she was willing to allow him to hold it. The coolness of the onyx stone, and the weight of it in his warm hands were pleasant. She placed it neatly back in its alcove and they all continued down the hallway.

Behind Rilke, Siena locked and secured windows and occasionally turned out a light. It seemed they had been walking for a while into the house, but it was really just a long hallway along the hillside. There were plants and stone sculptures or mosaics everywhere. There was art made with bicycle parts and he was amazed that no one had turned them in for scrap, but instead chose to make something colorful and artistic. Each time he thought they might be coming into a room, it was just a way station with a door into the mountain.

The occasional rock jutting into a room or into the hall reminded Rilke that whomever had built here did not remove but instead added to the dwelling as it already existed. He was fascinated but also familiar with scavenged structures. In the stadium, hives and hallways rose out of scrap plastic and cardboard or driftwood. A world created on the scaffolding and armature of past excesses. The kids of the stadium found the debris washed up along the asphalt landings. These might have once been parking garages, but now they were the best places to go after a storm.

Here in Siena and Florence's unwinding labyrinth of a home he felt safe, though. He did not have to worry about a storm surge, or watch the water levels through the night in case he had to signal an emergency. Already he knew he would sleep restfully without fearing the hurricanes that autumn often brought. He could hear the mountain's winds ripping against the ridge but he felt safe inside the Earthship, solid against the mountain.

After a few minutes, they came to the end in the hallway. The hall appeared to continue past them, but the passage had been filled with stone and brick. There was a mosaic made from many kinds of ceramic tile pieces that created a swirling deluge of blue. It continued along the wall leading toward and over an arch on his right.

"We have to go this way, now." Siena steered Rilke toward a small doorway through the arch. They climbed stairs that concluded in a dome-shaped structure. He could tell they were higher up than before and that this had been a newer construction by many years from where they had been before.

"There was a landslide in 2043. Instead of trying to repair the Earthship corridor, they just rerouted up. They crossed over the boulders to a stable rock table and built a structure here." Siena explained this difference as they entered a main room that felt like a foyer of sorts. Here, everyone sat on a curved bench and removed their shoes. Rilke didn't need to be told, he just watched what Siena and Florence were doing and followed suit. At first he was embarrassed because he was sure they would laugh at his shoes, but he saw that theirs were similar.

Florence talked more about the house as they sat in the golden anteroom where he could see a little of the room beyond. The cushioned seats were a plush velvet and he liked how they all sat for a moment while Florence talked and just rested. Even Fen relaxed and jumped up to sit beside Rilke and rest her head in his lap. She allowed him to pet her and he was grateful.

Florence's voice was musical, and enjoyably rhythmic, even when she was just providing details about the art on the wall or explaining how each new owner of this home had attempted some new construction, some new exploration of form and sustainability. They could not have predicted that the house would grow into what it was now, a sprawling museum of sorts, an origin point for the farm that Siena treasured.

A hundred years before, it had been a hostel, and people who had come to hike the mountain path had rented the rooms. They would work the farm and provide maintenance while waiting to begin the trip. But eventually their number would be called and they would embark northbound. At that time, they were motivated by the world of the deep forest and the flowing mountains that rippled up the continent.

Fen grew sleepy as Florence talked about the multiple intentional communities that had come and gone and the ecovillage that was partly boarded up, all their guests gone north already.

Rilke took in the warmth of the house from this small vestibule, eager to explore the glowing rooms that lit the interior. He had never been inside a home other than his bungalow or some semi-temporary structure awaiting the next storm. He had also never been inside the home of someone whom he didn't know. He had only ever seen the glimpse of light or heard the glimmer of sound.

But here Rilke was, preparing to enter the largest and most comfortably-furnished interior he'd ever seen. Around every corner there was something new to see. A painting, a statue, a chair. The woodwork on the windows was a warm burnished pine and it shone brightly. Some of the walls had small shelves where books or carved figures cast interesting shadows or reflected a warm light.

They walked past shelves of books that stretched from ceiling to floor and he became dizzy with the thought of reading them, and even more giddy at the thought of talking to someone who had already read them. He had never spoken with someone else about the poetry he read so continuously and affectionately. He read more quietly to himself now than when he had lived alone, before Fen. Had it only been a week? But every night he read and recited the same, sonorous chant of time and objects that brought the holy feelings down.

Florence had a way of making everyone feel comfortable immediately. She did not seem to judge anyone, except maybe Siena. Siena, she was especially hard on. But everyone else she coddled.

Rilke and Fen were led from the vestibule through a main room with shelves set into the wall. The books were arranged according to subject area and author. Rilke knew this because Florence spent a few minutes explaining how she came to live here with Siena.

"I'd been living in the library downtown for forty years. A lot of people don't realize that books need a lot of tending to."

Siena glanced at Rilke and shook her head slightly from side to side before winking. Rilke took that as a sign to just listen politely, and not question.

Fen's claws clicked lightly on the shiny concrete floor as they walked though the great room and into the kitchen. She was already looking for the best place to perch. She hopped up into a chair that turned out to be perfect. Her nose was a little above the plate on the table and she didn't have to move her head to see the eyes of anyone else.

The table was large and round, and could seat twelve to fifteen people. It was formed of two circle halves that had been separated apart from one another so that someone could stand in the middle and access everyone's plate from inside the circle. It was a clever design, she thought, given that humans often made much of who sat where and how important it was to see everyone when speaking, or if people were seen as equals of each other.

Once seated, a strange thing happened. Siena asked everyone to bow their heads, and then she fell into something that Fen told Rilke was a prayer. In it, she asked some greater being to bless the food and the hands that prepared it. Then she asked for the being to bless it to the nourishment of their bodies. But overall, the entire blessing felt more like a way of making people feel like they were welcome and included.

"Do people do this everywhere?" thought Rilke.

"Not everywhere," thought Fen. But then she remembered how Canto would sometimes become silent at the beginning of a meal and bow his head just a little. She always felt he was grateful over his food and aware in the same way Siena and Florence were now. She liked that about human beings. They were sometimes so dissimilar from each other and at other times, so alike.

"Canto always said a grateful thought was a building

thought. He said that when we thought only about what we wanted or needed, that tore us down." At the conclusion of the prayer, Rilke eagerly eyed the food that was uncovered before him. A large round shape with a brown glaze tempted him to lean forward in interest and excitement. It smelled incredible.

There were also small round potatoes like the ones they grew outside the stadium on the terraces. Then there was a stack of green beans that Florence called half-runners. Tiny tan legumes peeked out from the green pods. There were also different kinds of relishes and fruit preserves that Siena promptly began to settle atop her pile of food, which Rilke didn't even notice she had already spooned onto her plate. She moved fast, like Rilke's uncle always did. Florence, on the other hand, was much more concerned about her guests.

"Honey, you like lab ham? How about some new potatoes?" She was already slicing off a slab and had put two slices on his plate before he had time to answer. Then she went ahead and spooned a pile of the small buttery red potatoes with herbs beside the ham. He didn't have time to object even if he had meant to.

"I think Brynja would say these are good people, Fen." Rilke thought as he began to eat what Florence had placed in front of him, and then continued to offer him as he finished each heaping pile.

Even Fen found something she liked. There was olive oil on the table for dipping bread into, and she watched attentively as Florence poured some into a small plate for Rilke and then showed him how to tear the bread and smear it in the oil after it had been dusted with salt and herbs. When Florence saw that Fen was watching with ears turned forward and that every part of her body seemed to be leaning toward the oil like a magnet, Florence heard the thought.

"You want some oily bread?" Fen gave a quick nod, so excited was she about the oil, and Florence placed a chunk of bread on a small plate and began to pour the oil on the bread in front of Fen.

"Now you say 'when,'" Florence prompted, and gave a little giggle when she heard the word "when" in her imagination.

"This is still new for me," she said smiling. When she began to reach for the salt, Fen made a quirring purr that sounded like a whine and a laugh and that sounded like a "no."

Florence chuckled and looked from Fen to Rilke.

"She talk like that, too?" Rilke nodded and smiled. He liked the way Florence made an effort to know Fen and understand her. She did the same with him, but it made him happy to know she could do that for someone who was not human.

Brynja had understood what Fen was, but that also made her treat Fen as a kind of thing. It was so odd, how people saw her so differently than he did. How Siena, even now, pretended to not care too much about what the fox was doing while Florence admired her and lavished attention on her and Rilke in a nurturing way.

They all ate and chatted merrily while Fen chewed the bread and licked her plate. The time flew by until Siena stood up and placed her napkin along her plate. Rilke watched Florence for cues and Fen sat back on her haunches rolling her tongue across her nose in a satisfied, tired gesture that signaled "nap time" to everyone who was there.

"I'm going to the courtyard, I guess. You can join me if you like." Siena took her plate to the kitchen and walked out, leaving Florence, Rilke, and Fen at the table.

Rilke helped Florence take up the dishes into the kitchen

and wash them. He knew how to do this because he always helped with dishes in the stadium and sometimes at Kasim's bakery. Fen rested on a luxurious dog bed she found in the corner. She circled a few times before settling. Then she thought about the dog whose smell she could faintly grasp from the cushion where a bit of his scent remained. It was an old scent.

Fen could hear laughing as Florence and Rilke walked past her snoozing form on the cushion near the door. As they passed by she heard Florence unlock the dog door. Comforted by this, she drifted again into memory.

Mimi had come into the kitchen and passed through the short hallway to the bedroom where Canto lay, listless. She saw Fen there on the bed, near the corner, resting her head on her paws.

"Fen?" When she heard the woman, Fen looked up, ears to the side in cautious, curious greeting. She wagged her voluminous plume of a tail, which was almost larger than she was.

Fen was indigo, tinged with a light blue powder and an iridescent sheen that became nearly invisible on Mimi's hands as she ruffled the fox's cheeks and touched noses.

"How is he, my darling girl?" Fen whined in short bursts that sometimes trilled and other times sounded like a soft, chittering squeal of worry. As she did so, Mimi nodded her head and stroked Fen's head reassuringly.

"I know. He's sad." The color of the fox told her everything, but looking at Canto hurt Mimi to the quick. He was clearly ill.

Fen and Canto went to live with Mimi in her house. There had been doctors and whispers, the visits of friends. Gradually, Canto began to feel better and to respond when people said his name aloud and spoke to him. He began to be capable of response, and could say with some sincerity, "Thank you. I'm doing well, and you?"

This is all Mimi had wanted at first, but then she got greedy. She arranged for every joyful thing she knew he loved to be in close proximity to him, whether it be music, or a photo album, or a favorite scent. It was the winter, so there was a fire, and occasionally the smells of evergreen would drift through the house. And so it was that by degrees, ever so slowly, Canto came back to himself.

Canto had once told Fen that people wanted to be near him because he was always giving something away that they wanted. It was something they needed and he didn't, not really. And somehow Fen had come to understand that it was the central misery of his life to be wealthy.

Fen thought about Rilke in the courtyard with Florence and Siena. Siena saw her as "fox" or "the AI." She was technically neither, exactly. But given that she could feel and communicate, did those distinctions even matter? She had all of the characteristics of being alive and she also felt and knew things. She had been given abilities far past that of most animals but also beyond some human beings. In that shadowy intersection between what was shaped matter and sapience, she walked in the deepest of her dreams.

Fen heard the door open and close, quiet feet enter the kitchen, turn a faucet, collect water. The glass filled and a human was drinking. It was Florence, and she went back outside with a pitcher, walking silently past the dreaming Fen.

If Canto had been alone, he would have lain there in that bed and not eaten. He would have wasted away as he had been on his way to do before Mimi caught him. Mimi came and saw her neglected Fen at the corner of the bed, and knew she had to take Canto home. Maybe Rilke needed that too. Maybe Rilke had never had anyone to care, and he had been sad and alone but he didn't know it because he had nothing else to compare it too. But her purpose and meaning was ultimately to care for Canto. She wasn't sure yet how this moment connected to the moment when she would see him again.

Through scent, Fen had the ability to see this dog who had slept on the cushion every night and every morning of his life. He lived between the lives of these humans. He was sometimes the best part of their lives together, and never asked for anything. One day Siena had come home and found him, gently sleeping on the cushion like he had always done, but now not moving and not breathing. And she had wept like a little girl because she had loved him. She was glad he wasn't in any pain. The death of this dog had changed Siena and Fen felt it. Fen knew the grief was still in Siena, through the fact of this bed and the dog door that had remained locked for years until moments before.

Fen saw it all in her dreams, the way Siena needed to be comforted. Fen saw that this comfort was one way of getting home to Canto. To ensure the well-being of Rilke was to also be present for Siena and Florence. She nestled her snout into the ditch of her paws and sighed. She had so much to do before she could think about looking for Canto. And still, even now, she was at a loss for how to find him. This is why she needed Rilke, and now, Florence and Siena.

When Fen awoke she had the sensation of peace still covering her like a warm blanket. She felt it now, what Rilke had said earlier. These were good people. She could see them clearly through the old dog's memories, reveries of a kind. They were like dreams that have threaded their way into where someone sleeps. The dog was there in an elemental sense, in the material substance of the bed. But the dog was gone, so it was not a being she felt, but more like the memory of particles which called out to her in semblance. They seemed to say, "You who are also loved. We have been a loved-dog, we have been loved-cats, we have been loved and are love. Stay with us a while."

Fen knew that she and Rilke would be staying much longer than a few nights. She stood up, stretched her little fox body until a shiver cavorted to the tip of her tail, and leaped through the dog door into the courtyard. There, Rilke, Siena, and Florence sat in yard chairs circling an Edenic brick-lined yard.

They were laughing about a story that Florence told from her librarian days, and even though Fen didn't hear the story, she could tell that Rilke was relaxed and at home here, even after only a couple of hours. She liked seeing him around other human beings. He was someone who had a lot to learn about the world and these were people who could teach him the better parts of it, like Canto was able to teach her.

At the thought of Canto, she paused. What if he were gone? What if she never saw him again? It couldn't be true because he'd always been in control. When he was *well*, at least.

It was odd to her how someone could be powerful and wise, wealthy and good, but break at the slightest tune on the wind. He could see a news headline and fall into a slump for days. He might lie in bed, have his virtual assistants manage his calendars, and cancel his meetings. He could do that for a while, but then Mimi would inevitably show up, open the shades, and make him get up. She'd make her strong coffee for him and turn on some music. It was difficult for him to go against her medicine, which was at its plainest, love. He was okay with this for a while, but another blow would strike his empathic heart and lay him low.

"I'm glad to see you are happy." Fen came close to where Rilke sat and leaned against him affectionately.

Florence noted how cat-like Fen seemed, and Rilke agreed.

"She has memories of having been cats and dogs, too." When he said this, Siena coughed, stood up, and excused herself to the house. Florence was quiet for a moment and then explained.

"She's been lost without Webb. He was her best friend for almost twenty years. At some point she stopped taking him to the vet because she was afraid to cross a line. She had twenty good years with him as a dog with just a few edits. We think he passed away in his sleep peacefully, which was a kindness. She's been broken up by his death, even so." Florence looked at her hands, turned them over and looked back up, smiling at Fen.

"But you know that, don't you." Rilke was curious and looked over at Fen who had moved to casually claim Siena's empty seat.

"Yes. Much of him is still in the cushion. Not Webb, exactly, but his calm. The love he felt for Siena, also."

"I think she might need to hear that at some point. She always wondered if she should have had him scanned and recorded, but she never felt right about it. Said it was wrong to keep only a mimicry of Webb alive just to satisfy her desire to live in the past."

"I think it's more complicated than that for her, though," Fen projected toward Florence. Rilke understood the context of the thought, without knowing its specifics.

"Siena doesn't trust Fen. Is it because she is a fox or

because she can talk?" he asked Florence.

"I don't think it's either of those things. She's just more attached to the land and to the natural progression of a life than she is to what human beings can create. She allowed just enough intervention to keep Webb going into the outer edges of a dog's potential lifespan. But no more. At the point where we are replacing parts of him, we are taking those parts from him, she always said. I respected her feelings on this and I did not interfere. But sometimes I wish I'd encouraged her to have a memory pin cast. She might not have regretted so much then, even if she never used it."

"I have memories of cats and of dogs. I am not sure sometimes who or where I am, but I remember. And I can see people who have always been with me, but at different ages and from different angles. Sometimes I am jumping into a lap as a cat, luxurious in my fluidity. But then I also recall running, so fast the wind could have carried me many meters off the ground." She looked at both of them and saw that they were listening.

"Once, I was running through the grasses and they whipped my face as I ran. My tongue lolled in delight, and the wind dried the roof of my mouth. The taste of the scents I pursued were already fading, but then they became me." Fen continued.

"I remember the exuberance of catching the ball, of bringing it back, of wanting to do it again and again. I remember rolling in the fresh cut grass. Who am I to say where these thoughts and feelings end in me? They are me. Sometimes I am small. Sometimes I am slow. But they are all me." She paused and Florence nodded in response.

Fen was able to share the thought with Florence and Rilke because both were so open and receptive to her. She felt secure, and for the first time she began to rest, to sit back and watch each human as they understood her. Both were natural empaths. But Fen knew Siena would be a difficult and skeptical listener. Siena would likely insist that it was programming, and not memory, that Fen related.

But Fen remembered Mimi, a young Mimi, and her life as a fox had begun when Mimi was an older woman crossing one hundred years old. Canto's thirty years had all been recorded too. He was the one who threw the ball to her on summer days spent by the lake. She liked those memories as a dog best because they were fun and lighthearted. He must have been ten? She was an old dog by then and memory pins were still new. The dog was still a recording only, and perhaps a template of sensation, embedded into the consciousness of a different dog. Maybe that's why she didn't remember the cat until she was Fen. Somehow the fox bridged the two.

Fen knew that she had almost been enough, but Mimi was really the one who pulled Canto out of the depression that nearly killed him. Fen had been lost, watching over Canto's sleep without a plan. All she could do was feel Canto's internal silence, woven through his mind and into the sanctum of his heart.

Siena took Rilke and Fen with her to walk the farm a few days later.

Over breakfast, she had explained that it was not a good idea to start the walk on the Narrow Road until early spring. She also clarified that there would be biometric processing at the end. This, she said, was where the real value was, because no one wanted to get that far north just before winter and be looking for a way into Canada. No one could enter Canada without biometric surveys, and no one left the American States without authorization. Narrow Road travelers were already authorized and in the system.

All of this sounded frightfully complex to Rilke who seemed stressed until Siena leveled with him.

"Look. This is actually pretty simple. You walk all the way to Mount Katahdin and someone there will drive you to the outbound processing station. They check to see that you walked the entire way North, that you checked in at way stations, that you were supported along the way. But you have to follow their rules, and one of the first is that only I can clear you to walk. And you are not cleared to walk, not before I've helped you prepare."

He finally understood that there were trade-offs. He could enjoy the support of two national governments, or he could make the trip impossible. There were rules to follow, just as there had been in Savannah.

Fen, on the other hand, was impatient.

"What do you mean, we have to wait?" For a week they had lounged about, eating and talking and getting haircuts or making new clothes or shoes. It was useful and important, but she wanted reassurance that they would eventually be on the way to Canto.

Even after Rilke explained everything to her, she was frustrated. But there was the matter of weather. When Siena explained that they had to carry everything that they would need along the way, that there weren't hostels every five miles and that some sections might have been closed in the past decade without notice due to floods, landslides, or wildfires, Fen began to see the seriousness of Siena's argument.

She would not see Canto until potentially the fall of the coming year. Trains were costly, and unless they wanted to hobo their way to the Canadian border, it was walking all the way. The roads were not reliably kept, and most people did not have a vehicle capable of making a cross county trip north for just one person and a fox.

"Besides," said Siena as they walked along the edge of her pawpaw orchard, "you want the free processing benefits, the free shelters and hostels in the Narrow Road network. You can't afford this otherwise."

She pointed at some scat on the ground. "Fen, can you tell me how fresh this is?"

Fen approached the semi-dried pile that had a number of seeds worked through it and did her best to think like a fox, and not like a pampered house cat. She also realized it would be useless to try and communicate the complexities of what she smelled to the others, so a summary would have to do.

"Sometime yesterday, maybe sixteen hours."

Siena was satisfied by the answer and asked another question.

"Do you know where it was headed?"

At this point, Fen felt most strongly the connection that had been between Siena and Webb. This was one of the memory dreams she recalled from napping on Webb's cushion. Siena would point to something, and then ask Webb this very question. And somehow, simple creature that he was, he knew to follow the scent as it wound its way along the edges of pastures and fallow fields, staying always to the trees and shrubs that concealed his shape. Webb could see the bear with his imagination. It was because of his nose and the data gathering that happened there that he could retrace that same walk, but in a way that the human could follow.

Webb wanted to help Siena, always, with so much great love in his heart. Not just because she fed him and gave him a cushion by the door, or a door at all. It was not the belly rubs or treats, or even the truck rides to bring people with new smells on them from far away. It was because he loved her and he knew she loved him.

For about a week, Rilke had trouble sleeping at Siena and Florence's farm. The room that he and Fen shared was comfortable, but that wasn't the problem. It was *too* comfortable and he worried that he was going to sink into the bed and never want to come out or that he would hurt the sheets or the bedspread, so tenderly did he regard them.

He marveled at the continuously hot water and enjoyed being able to look forward to a day spent outside on the farm, not looking over his shoulder or knocking on doors. It was nice to feel clean, to have pajamas, to have people who wished him goodnight. There were so many things he feared growing used to. The comfort, the safety, the peace.

"Canto's room and bed are like this, only . . . much better in ways you wouldn't be able to understand." Fen went ahead and answered the question that Rilke had not asked, but must have relayed without thinking. She had jumped up on the corner of the bed and was beginning to circle down for the night.

"What do you mean?" he thought back towards her swiftly, a bit uncomfortable that so much of his mind was now open to her in ways he could not control. Worse, it was becoming easier to communicate back to her through thought rather than with speech, and that was awkward too. Sometimes he said things to Siena or Florence and then realized he had merely thought the words. This had led to many small confusions.

Rilke climbed into bed and fluffed the comforter, marveling at the loft. Never had he enjoyed such a wondrous thing. How poofy! He pressed his hands into the top of the blanket again and again to test the softness. He glanced down at Fen who was still settling, but noticed that it took her more time than usual. She fell into a curled position and tightened her tail around her, even though there wasn't a draft and she was nestled in the blanket and backed against a pillow. It was like she was hugging herself with her tail and in an instant, she was the same emerald green as the blanket.

Rilke also noted for the first time that perhaps Fen was unhappy, but he wasn't sure why. She had been treated respectfully and kindly ever since they had arrived and even Siena had warmed up a bit, calling Fen by her name instead of "the fox" or "the wildlife unit." Everyone had also agreed that the word "AI" was offensive and wouldn't be thrown about lightly, and certainly not applied to anyone living at the farm. Rilke was sure that Florence had something to do with that last realization.

But there was something else under the surface. The more that he pondered, the more he was also aware that Fen knew his questions already. That brought him back around to something he had wanted to ask Fen since they first met. He shifted his head on the pillow and looked up at the ceiling. Someone had painted stars there. They glowed faintly, but he knew that when he turned out the lamp they would glow even brighter. He thought about reaching for his book of poems, but worried the pages might fall out again. He would go up to Florence's tower in the morning and see if she could fix the book.

"Were there ever times when you *weren't* listening in on Canto's thoughts?" Rilke did not intend to blurt out the question but he was also earnestly curious about the limitations of his privacy. He also felt a bit jealous of Canto, and doubtful that anyone could have a bed more comfortable than the one he was in.

It was a new and also contradictory impulse to shield his

thoughts and feelings, to guard them, but also to share them. He preferred the conversations he had with Siena and Florence in some ways because he could choose what he thought and what he said. He could not choose when he was with Fen, not without effort, and switching back and forth between communicating with her and speaking with other humans was disorienting.

Fen lifted her head. "It's something you have control over but it takes time to develop. And in some ways you have to close out that part of your empathy that unconsciously wants to connect whether or not you want to." Fen saw this principle clearly, but then she had lived with Canto and Mimi long enough to develop some balance.

Sometimes Canto shielded his thoughts from her. Sometimes Mimi did too. But she knew when to search their faces and when to leave them to their private thoughts. Sometimes, it was just better if she weren't around at all. Occasionally, Canto asked Fen to "visit the moon," as he liked to call it. That was their code for alone time, or alone-with-another-human-time.

When Canto had a special guest over, Fen would sometimes go to Mimi's part of the house and sit with her. But even Mimi sometimes drew boundaries, especially when she realized that Canto was busy, and Fen had just come by to see her out of boredom.

"Shoo, you naughty fox!" Mimi would sometimes playfully chide. She would pretend that Fen was a wild animal and throw pillows at her. Fen would chitter and laugh while running around the room, knocking lamps over and shaking cushions until their stuffing would pop out.

Then she would run through the room like a bullet and ricochet from the wall to the upper terrace where a small door opened to the gardens. There she would hide until Mimi lured her back inside with cheese wedges and warm yeast rolls. Then Fen would slink back to the comfort and safety of the house and chew the cheese and rolls blissfully, loving the way the cheese stuck to her teeth and extended the flavor. The rolls were always soft and buttery, and she liked how they cleaned her teeth of the cheese but also made everything more wonderful with their warmth and substance.

Afterward, sometimes she would run around in circles after her tail in Mimi's day room or push her snout along the freshly trimmed grounds of the gardens to store the grassy green odor in her whiskers. After that, Mimi would call the assistant, and there would be a bath. Fen liked the attention more than anything.

But Fen didn't think of these things much any more. There was no point to her wishing for a life that was gone. She looked at Rilke, his curly head propped up on three pillows, as he began to squeeze his face into a grimace as if he'd licked a lemon.

"How about now."

Fen stared at him blankly. "What are you doing?"

"Trying to close you out of my head." Rilke looked as if he might be in pain.

Fen sighed and rolled her eyes. "I know when you want privacy. And you can always just ask me to leave." Fen felt a pang of an emotion she didn't like and she hoped it would go away.

"Would I tell you to 'visit the moon'?" He looked at her with a smirk and Fen felt yet another feeling she didn't like, but another one she did. There was an irony there and she appreciated Rilke's quickness.

"Looks like you're catching on," she snorted. "But this is what I mean; if you are open and receptive, it's easier for me to understand. If you are trying to hide something from me, you can learn to do that. But sometimes I will know things, not because you told me with your thoughts, but because I sense things. I am an organic being." Fen raised her chin proudly.

Rilke remembered the moment on the train, when he felt that the man in the dining car had intentions he did not understand. But Rilke had remained open and empathetic without protecting himself. He had not wanted to believe that such a harmless-seeming man could be dangerous.

Brynja's parting words had been about something similar to what Fen was saying now, about closing one's self to other people. She had looked into Rilke's eyes with something like concern.

"Sometimes you need to put on your armor, Rilke. It's a matter of survival." Then she was gone from the compartment and Fen had leaned against Rilke to reassure him. They watched Brynja from the window as she stepped from the train to the platform, and disappeared into the station's teeming interior. Then the train had begun to chuff and screech and soon they were alone once more.

The next morning, Rilke took his book of poems in hand and went to find Florence. Though he had memorized most of the poems already, he still liked having the book as a comfort. But lately, it had been coming undone, falling from its cover, completely unglued. He had to wrap it in cloth and tie it with string to keep it together.

He also desperately hoped to read something new. Most of Siena's books were downstairs and about subjects like pruning and compost. They didn't interest him as much as Florence's infamous library, which he had not yet seen.

The first few days had been about getting oriented. He had learned the lay of the house and he had learned the courtyard and the orchards closest by. He and Fen fed the chickens who had their run of the place until nightfall. Sometimes he hung out with Siena while she milked the goats, and he even learned how. Fen had been appalled.

But Florence had been busy much of the days on her own, and Rilke was curious. He was hoping she would help him fix the book and maybe lend him something else to read.

First he knocked, and when no one answered, he went on in. Siena had said it was okay to do this since Florence was usually on the top floor. He climbed the stairs in what Siena referred to as "Florence's Tower," a three-story, hard-sided yurt with a winding staircase. The interior wall was lined with an undulating shelf that wound its way up to the top floor, filled with books on every subject and increasing in number as he approached the upper level.

"Hello?" Rilke stopped below the first step and called out.

"Come on up," He found her at a small desk with a pair of scissors in her hand. She appeared to be dismembering a large tan book that was filled with colorful images.

Seeing Rilke's horror, she chuckled. She gestured for him to sit beside her, which he did, clutching his dear book of poems to his chest.

"Now, now. This book's spine is already broken. And it's too big. There's no chance that anyone will ever look inside this book so I'm taking the images out where people can see them." Rilke looked skeptical, but then he could see paintings and sketches all around the room that had surely come from the same book.

"Vincent Van Gogh. There's an intensity to his work I've always liked, and I'll never see the real paintings anyway. Might as well enjoy them here and now." Florence flipped through, looking at one page then turning a few more before pausing again. Then she stopped and sat back so she could talk to Rilke.

"So what have you brought me?" She lowered her glasses and looked at him before glancing down and noticing that Fen wasn't with him. "And where's your shadow?"

Rilke hesitated but lay the book down in front of her. She took the cue from his eyes and set her scissors down too, but far from his book of poetry.

"Fen's walking the orchard with Siena. I brought my book . . . I can't turn the pages." He looked at her as if his book were a bird with a broken wing, and she, a butcher, who had been carving up a larger bird moments before.

"Let's take a peek." Very gently, she unwrapped the book, and lifted the pages one by one, tutting every once in a while before turning to the next page and then the next. Rilke distracted himself again by looking at the roof timbers and the words in other languages that were painted on the ceiling. Some words looked familiar, but most of them were unknown to him.

Florence caught his gaze and looked up too. "The quotations? Those are meant to be like the ones in Montaigne's study. You know him?" She looked at Rilke over her glasses, then shook her head. "I'm guessing not." She sighed and pulled her glasses off before gently closing the book and looking at Rilke.

Florence had once been a lifelong book tender, and when her library was decommissioned, she was offered the books and phonograph archives as a kind of peace offering. In her tower, she was like a queen, as much as Siena was when out on her farm moving hay or feeding the sheep. Outside, Siena's world made her seem taller and stronger. It was the same here, but it was Florence's books that made her formidable and expert in her ruminations.

Rilke feared the worst. Perhaps there was nothing to be done. "I just thought you might be able to help," he said morosely, looking down at the snipped pages she'd already cut pictures out of. He didn't know how to ask to borrow a book when he had obviously taken such poor care of his own. But then here she was cutting a book into pieces and making it . . . not a book at all. Maybe he shouldn't ask for anything to read.

"Oh, I can fix it, sugar. There's a fella in Boston I mail books to and he makes them new again. No, I'm just concerned about this awful translation. Is this all you been reading?" Relieved, Rilke let out a breath that made Florence clap him on the back in good humor.

"We'll make sure you have plenty to read for as long as you're here. I'll send the book up and we might get it back by spring. Sound good?"

Rilke was noticeably cheered by her offer of books. "You mean there's more than one book of his poems?"

"Child, there's a lot of poetry in the world. You might even find something you like better. Let's at least get you reading some different translations. Maybe some Stephen Mitchell? Or C.F. MacIntyre?" She stood up and Rilke did the same. Before he knew it she had loaded him up with three bags of books. Some on history, which he had asked for, and also a book on mountains. She slipped in another book about hiking and bid him set his books near the top of the stairs.

"You ever heard a record player?"

He shook his head, but then caught himself. "You mean music? Someone had a radio in the stadium. We knew when storms were coming. There was singing some nights and we listened."

"But you never chose what to listen to?"

"No ma'am." He was curious.

Florence led him to one side of the room where boxes organized hundreds of albums. In a moment she had placed a gleaming plate on a spinning circle and had set the needle down. The result was a revolution of sound. A riot of impulses. To move, to listen, to live within the aura of voice and feeling that emerged from the ebony disk.

"That's how I like learning about the past, most of the time." She winked at Rilke and left the album to play.

Returning to her table, she wrapped up Rilke's book, careful to place it near the ones she was sending for repair. She wrote Rilke's name on a slip of paper and placed it under the string holding the book together.

Then she took up her scissors and looked back at her massive volume of Van Gogh's paintings and sketches. Rilke wandered near her and watched, enjoying the light streaming in from the skylight and the cool mountain breeze from the window, as well as the music on the archaic machine. Florence hummed lightly to herself as she worked.

She considered which side of the page was her favorite. There was a delicious finality to her choosing, an acceptance of change and loss. The insides of books, the interesting part, was invisible, except to the people with faith and knowledge in equal supply. This had always bothered her.

Florence decided on an image and decided it would look nice in the foyer. It was one of her favorites, and she'd meant to cut it out a long time ago but hadn't. In the painting, which might have just been a study, a figure seemed to be sowing. Their right arm extended behind them, and the left was propped on their hip. Maybe they were just walking across the grape-colored field with the lemony sun in the background, almost bigger than the figure walking, the texture of the rays hard and sharp and thick against the golden orange of the wheat below and the brightness of the morning.

Florence looked at Rilke and saw he was studying the image too. "Is it morning or evening, you think?" He shook his head and she began to cut the painting out of the book, thoughtful and silent in her work.

The record flipped itself over and the needle found the groove of the B-side. Rilke became mesmerized by the drifts of strings, their sounds wafting through the autumn light. That same light cast gold around Florence's contemplation, rendering the destruction of the art book forgivable and necessary, like a harvest.

In the image, both distant and meditative, floating on the bed of wheat, a gray-blue farmhouse with a terra-cotta roof. Two spindly trees. Somewhere hot and dry? Three birds of licorice landing behind the walker, in a furrow that the walker ignores. Maybe no one is planting seeds, but just walking through and across, on their way somewhere else.

Memory

Siena awoke in a sweat, and walked to the kitchen to pour herself a glass of water. Florence was sleeping soundly, so she didn't disturb her. But she needed to think.

Siena had the dream again, the one where she returned home after the bear attack and found Webb, bloodied, whining under the porch. Despite her fear of snakes, she had crawled to him. With a sheet, Siena and Florence had managed to lift him out so she could rush him to the vet.

It was difficult on those nights to remind herself that the attack had not killed Webb, but had helped the dog develop a healthy fear of black bears. They were common in this part of the country, and Siena had always anticipated the possibility of a bear attack until it actually happened. Then it was a shock she was not prepared for. There were stitches and a long recuperation period where Webb spent more time sleeping on the cushion than he had before. He would stare out the glass window into the courtyard before limping outside, even though he knew nothing could harm him in the enclosed space.

But the dreams were worse than the actual event, because in them sometimes Webb was killed instead of injured, and after those dreams Siena woke up stricken with the loss of Webb all over again. It was as if there were a parallel reality where Webb had died then, and all those good years that had followed were gone. Except Webb really was gone, and Siena still struggled to accept the truth. She waited for the day when the big golden dog would lope in through the door again and their lives could go on as they had before.

Siena reached for some of Florence's lemonade and sat at the table, alone in the dark. She had loved that dog. He was her child, her best friend, sometimes even a teacher. He helped her interact with people. He helped her laugh. He reminded her that she was important, at least in his world.

There must have been some kind of hound in him, she sometimes thought. He was somewhere between a retriever and a pointer, perhaps also with a bit of shepherd thrown in. Gratefully, he was decades into a culture more tolerant of spectrums and blends than generations before, and though there were still purebred dogs, a lot of the genetics had been perfected. This allowed for an endless calibration of breed characteristics without wasteful experimentation.

Siena sipped the lemonade and thought about dogs. Maybe it was time to move on? She shook her head. Nah, there would be no way to get what she wanted in a dog as long as what she wanted was Webb. Healthy. Not verbose, like the resident augmented fox. For some reason she had never seen the rationale of a fox as a pet. Far too rowdy. They would pee in your shoes if they loved you. They would eat all of the couches and strew the stuffing across two floors. Why anyone would prefer that wildness over a good old American mutt was beyond her. No, there was no replacing Webb, not even with a lab-hound-shepherd mix like he was.

If she did find a dog, who would this one be? Would she write to one of her contacts in Vermont? She and Florence could take the fast train up, bring the dog back in a couple of days. Ha! Like she could ever leave the farm. Whatever travel she used to enjoy was a thing of the past.

Siena put the cup in the sink and tapped the light. She crawled back into bed and nestled up against Florence's back. A dog would bring nothing but heartache.

One afternoon, Siena said it was time for a walk, and no one argued. Already, the weather was changing and the nights were cooling. The four of them relaxed into a steady pace along an old road between fields, breaking rank only to leap over puddles or move fallen branches. Conversation was easy with Rilke and Fen springing lightly ahead and then running back, or walking with Florence or Siena and asking questions about plants or animal tracks. Occasionally one of them would find a rock and Rilke would run it over to Siena for identification.

Fen loved finding rocks, and was closest to the ground. She had even managed to find an old arrowhead and some flint knapping shards near the creek in the rich bottom land. Siena was amazed that they were finding such old artifacts. But she was unwilling to acknowledge that the fox was the one who discovered them each time.

Fen knew that Siena didn't like her, but she also knew the feeling was complicated. It wasn't just a dislike based on her being augmented, but because Fen represented everything that Siena did not choose for Webb. Fen's memory was built on the brains of past animals, recorded then replicated in her, a unit not fully organic, nor machine exactly. She was a synthesis, and Siena was not someone who wanted a synthesis. She wanted the essential dog himself, Webb, as he was then, and only him, not a memory or an implant. But there was also a strange guilt, as if she regretted not ever trying.

Fen was careful to not bring these observations into conversation. She could sense them, just under the surface of Siena's conscious thought. The fox was crossing a line by digging deeper into Siena's thoughts, but she also couldn't help trying to understand.

Rilke and Florence were busy looking at the sunset as Fen and Siena passed them by, sharing thoughts. Fen thought it funny that the person most confused by her existence was also the one who spoke more readily through thought than words. Siena appreciated the ease of their communication, and perhaps also didn't want Rilke and Florence to see her speaking aloud to Fen. She didn't want them to think they were friends, because they certainly weren't. Siena was trying to help Fen see why a memory pin would not have worked.

It wasn't enough to have the being that was "Webb" installed in a close copy. It would not do for this creature that was not Webb to have all of his memories. To Siena, that was a false and terrible junction of technology and nature. She did not want the simulation, however realistic-seeming it could have been. She struggled with the death of Webb because it was truly a death of everything he was and had been. Their relationship only existed if he had also existed, and borrowing his memory for some new dog, even a clone, was not right by her thinking. You either were, or were not. There was no afterlife of memory or genetic perfection to be had, if it was to be real. And for Siena, everything had to be real, crystal clear, and open.

"Is this why you chose to work for the census?"

Siena nodded. "I wanted to make sure that people who chose to walk were really up to it. It's not something to embark upon lightly." Siena picked up a branch across the path and tossed it over to the field's edge. She continued, impressing on Fen what she saw as the truth of it. "Most people would be better off to settle, work on some farm or another or build their own. It would even be better to take a short-term rail porter contract than walk the Narrow Road."

Fen stopped. "Do you think Rilke can do this?" Fen glanced away to ensure that Florence and Rilke were still looking at the orange sky and deep in conversation. Then she peered up at Siena intently.

Siena pretended to tie her shoe and leaned down. "Yes, but you need to wait until late March, maybe even April. It's winter in those mountains even when it's summer here. Especially once you get further up, you understand?" She stood up, but continued to stare down at Fen with a stern expression. It was uncomfortable to be looked at this way, but Fen understood. Siena was concerned about Rilke, and protective, perhaps even as much as she had been of Webb.

"But he'll make it, right? We'll see Canto by September?" Siena did the unexpected, which was to come down to where Fen was, on one knee. The tall woman looked at the fox and held her chin gently, as if Fen were a dog or a child.

"Hey, he can make it. But listen here—" Siena locked gazes with the fox and said this last part slowly as she stared into Fen's face. "He's not like you. He doesn't see threats and danger. He sees only good people and nice chatty animals. Not because he's been privileged like you, but because he is naive, and new to the world. People take advantage of that. Nature will take advantage of that. You hear me? You keep him safe, little fox."

And then the woman stood up and stalked away on her

own back toward the house. The air was no longer golden, but cool, and Fen could scent the raccoons and hear the owls and the squirrels all singing their evening songs of the woods and fields. Somewhere a pack of coyotes yipped that night was coming, and Fen shivered.

As she walked back to the house, Siena wondered if she had been too hard on Fen. But Siena had begun to realize that she was guarding her heart from future hurt. A preemptive approach to heartbreak.

Siena remembered one fall day in particular, once in late October, walking through the tree farm. The light had that autumn cast, as if the entire Earth was passing under a shadow in order to emerge in brighter light. Siena looked off toward the mountain and remembered that day long in the past when her grandfather had passed away. The mountain there had looked almost like this one, still coated in dazzling oranges and reds from the ridge and down along the slopes. Then it had cooled rapidly and she felt the sadness of his passing for the first time, in her bones.

But it had been the spring when she had lost Webb. She had walked up to this ridge and looked down into the valley, imagining his spirit chasing some quarry into the shadowy coves. Webb was continuing on without her in this vision, running into the day of his dying eager to see what it might bring. And she had to see it this way, always as something he chose for himself and not the harsh reality of death. She had smelled the wet creek where he had loved to play, and she had heard the spring peepers. New life in the face of loss.

Siena looked back to see the fox had joined Florence and Rilke and the three of them were walking more slowly now, as if trying to make the evening last as long as possible. It was similar to Siena's wish, that the winter carry on as long as possible, to delay Rilke and Fen from starting out unprepared.

"Come on, slow pokes!" She shouted after them. But she stood patiently, content. No one hurried. They still drug on, slower than Christmas. But she liked it. They weren't even trying to resist her prodding but they naturally slowed down even more. By the time they reached where she was standing, they were laughing and their faces were florid with joy and the heat of walking. The fox, on the other hand, looked somewhat downcast and tried not to show it. Instead she pretended to look for rocks on the ground, and trotted on toward the house past Siena, alone.

It was a quiet evening, a few weeks later, and the whole house was still recovering from Thanksgiving. There had been every kind of vegetable and fruit, multiple breads and pies, as well as a simulated turkey with stuffing that had three different kinds of mushrooms. But the pie, oh the pie. Rilke was delighted to learn there were other kinds of pies in the world. Pumpkin had become a new favorite, and it reminded him of a sweet potato pie his mom had made once in the stadium.

Because it had been a good year for canning, Florence was trading with Sangreave's wife. He was headed over in a bit to pick up the basket of canned goods, and Rilke figured that Fen would stay upstairs in the room they shared. But Fen lingered for a while longer in the kitchen, enjoying a final piece of pie.

"The last of it!" Florence announced to the house though she could not imagine Rilke would be able to stomach another morsel himself. But Fen had appeared first, shifting her weight excitedly from one forefoot to the other while Florence unceremoniously scooped the remnants into her bowl at the table. When the fox had finished the pie she looked up at Florence with gratitude and licked her lips. She trotted into the other room for some cold water from the new cat fountain just as a knock came from the side porch door. Sangreave had come through the courtyard and there wasn't time to hurry Fen upstairs.

Siena, coming from a different room, opened the door to Sangreave, a thin but straight-backed man with a huge smile and wild hair that was stark white when he took his hat off. He squinted when he saw Rilke and for a moment, Rilke wasn't sure if it was because Sangreave didn't see well or if his smile was so broad it left no space for any other expression. The man's cheerfulness filled the room like a bright, warm light, but this was all a bit too much for people used to sitting in the quiet dark.

"My boy, good to meet you!" The old farmer stuck out his hand good-naturedly and grabbed Rilke's so forcefully in a handshake that Rilke gasped with surprise.

"And who's this?" Sangreave bent down, and for a moment, Rilke's heart stuck in his throat. Sangreave had already gone down on one knee and was scratching Fen around the ears and roughhousing with her snout. She had applied the domesticated canine glamour.

Rilke couldn't believe what he was seeing. Instead of the orange-red coat of a fox, she was a beautiful rich brown. Her face and ears even appeared more doglike in the dim light of the kitchen. But that wasn't all. Her tail seemed thinner, more diminished from the massive brush that normally extended behind her cat-sized form. He had never seen her look so passive either. She allowed her tongue to loll out of her mouth and she panted enthusiastically, rolling her eyes goofily around at Siena and Rilke. It was a performance. Fen seemed to laugh in her amber eyes, and added, "Humans only see what they want to see," for Rilke's benefit.

The illusion must have been convincing because Sangreave decided that she was the "prettiest little bitch" he'd ever seen, and said that he knew a fella down the road who had a spitz, a purebred Icelandic sheepdog male. But it was when he said "I bet this bitch would whelp some fine pups," that Fen scaled back on her playfulness. Rilke could hear her cringing in anger, but she wagged her tail quickly and perfunctorily before she trotted out of the room to process what Sangreave had suggested.

Rilke and Florence both smiled politely but knew exactly how irritated the fox was. Neither of them said a word but watched Fen leave the room in helpless discomfort.

Siena cleared her throat and skillfully diverted the conversation. "Rilke here is planning to hike the Narrow Road with his dog come spring, so maybe pups will have to wait a while."

The old man appeared disappointed and Rilke decided that he was probably imagining a pile of fluffy pups with upright triangular ears and bushy tails. The thought was fun for about two seconds until he heard Fen protest from the other room in the space of his mind. It was the kind of thing that no one needed to push too hard on, and he respected her disgust.

Fen didn't even allow the word "vixen" to be used around her. She insisted that she didn't have the desire to mate or be anything but herself, and Rilke could relate to her feelings. He had never liked to be called "boy" or "kid" or "son," and sure enough, Sangreave fell into the pattern that many old Southerners did. But Sangreave wasn't trying to be insulting, and Rilke was a guest in Siena's house, so he withheld his comments, and kept smiling politely. He and Fen would likely stay up late talking about it, so at least he wasn't alone.

"It's good to meet you, son. Siena said there was new folks staying with her up here. You are always welcome at the house. The missus makes a mean butterscotch pie." At the mention of pie, Rilke perked up.

Sangreave took a basket from Florence that was filled with jars of green beans and canned vegetable soup. The old man cheerfully put his hat back on and waved goodbye to everyone. As an afterthought, he added, "I might have some work for you if you want to earn some coin for your trip." And then he was out the door, and gone as quick as he came.

Despite the frustration that Rilke and Fen had felt during their first introduction to Sangreave, they both agreed that coin was good and it might be fun to get out of Siena's house for a while. She had recently begun finding separate chores for them, so the dream of lazing about the house was done. Plus, she sometimes got angry when the truck wouldn't start or something had eaten a crop she'd been excited for, and she was a trifle scary when she began to curse. Everyone tended to slink away and hide during these moments and there were only so many excuses one could make to invade Florence's tower. Besides, Siena always found them there anyway.

Rilke and Fen chose to ride in the back of Siena's truck to the end of Sangreave's farm and walked in from there. They both relished the wind, Rilke through his curls and Fen through her fur. Siena drove slow and the sunlight dappled the light around them. Fen stood up on her forepaws behind the rear window and pushed her nose around so she could see what Siena saw as she drove. Fen felt fast when the wind flew around her ears. Rilke lay his head along the warm sides of the truck bed and shut his eyes, listening to the low rumble of the engine.

Sangreave was recovering from an injury after falling off his roof, and it felt right to help in whatever way they could. Siena had said something about him being "tough as a pine knot," but it was still a good thing they did, she said. "And he pays well," she added. She gave them a brief wave and headed down to the post office to hear the news and get the mail for people in the hollow.

The sun was a brilliant ember in the sky as Fen and Rilke trudged up the dusty path to old man Sangreave's farm. The shimmering heat of late summer in northern Georgia had finally given way to autumn, and it was crisp and cool by nightfall. The relentless chorus of insects had been growing fainter day by day.

"What do you think he'll have us working on?" Fen shifted into a dark brown color to appear more doglike.

"We're about to find out," Rilke wiped sweat from his brow as they approached the weathered barn. Inside they saw stacks upon stacks of wood. They were here to help with the looming task of preparing for winter.

As Rilke worked, the rhythmic thud of logs being stacked filled the air. Rilke's muscles burned with exertion. He glanced occasionally at Fen, who was carefully selecting wood, and admired how she managed to carry or drag a small log whenever she was able.

But the time went quickly and there hadn't been that many logs, really. By the end, Sangreave had wandered over and tried to help a bit too. He was incapable of not working, even with an injury.

"Enough for today, I reckon," Sangreave called out as shadows grew long across the yard. He was a silhouette against the setting sun, leaning heavily on his cane. His foot was wrapped up. "You and your dog are good workers! That's a good girl . . ." He leaned down and gave her a couple pats on the head.

Fen rolled her eyes at Rilke. By now the masquerade had stopped being funny to her. Apparently Siena had said something about using the "B" word around Rilke, whom (she lied) had a sensitivity to cursing cause he'd been raised by good Christian folk. When Sangreave heard this he had burst out in guffaws because he knew how much Siena cursed. But he also changed how he referred to Fen, "the little spitz," and began inviting Rilke to church every Sunday. At some point Rilke would have to go. But the promise of Sunday dinner at Sangreave's followed by butterscotch pie was a lure.

"I'm glad to rest before Siena arrives. She'll just have more work for us at the house," Rilke dropped onto a hay bale just inside the barn. Fen joined him, her tail flicking away a persistent fly. Sangreave headed into the barn office to phone Florence while Rilke and Fen lost themselves in silent reverie.

A whimper cut through the evening calm, pulling Rilke from his half-rested state. He sat up, listening intently. Fen perked up, her ears twitching toward an area of the barn further in.

"Did you hear that?" Rilke asked, standing up. "Let's check it out." They moved toward the interior, the quiet sounds drawing them deeper inside. Their eyes adjusted to the patchy darkness peppered with shafts of mote-rich light. The whimpers grew louder, more insistent.

"Over here," Rilke whispered, edging toward the tack room to reveal the source of the noise. Fen's nostrils picked up the scent of new life, a musky sweetness that mingled with the hay and old wood. Underneath the warm glow of a light, a litter of puppies squirmed against their mother's belly, their bodies pulsating with each breath. The mama was a retriever mix and after looking up quickly to see who was there, she laid her head back down. She seemed unconcerned and let out a relaxed sigh as Fen and Rilke approached.

"Look at them." Rilke whispered, his gaze softening as he stepped closer to the whelping box. "They're so small."

"Like fat little dumplings," the fox responded in Rilke's mind, her amber eyes capturing the scene with wonder. She had never seen puppies before.

Rilke knelt down, his fingers itching to touch the velvety fur but restraining out of respect for the mother's comfort. The puppies were a tangle of limbs and tails. Something in Rilke's chest tightened.

The puppies wriggled, nudging each other for a better spot against their mother's warmth. One caught Rilke's attention—a feisty one with a patch of white curls standing out against its light-yellow throat. It pushed its siblings aside with determined paws, its mouth opening in a silent yawn.

"Look at that one," Rilke pointed. "Spirited."

"Perfect and new." Fen wanted to touch him with her nose and breathe in his wee puppy scent, but she stayed back. The mother dog was aware Fen was no dog and there was a thin line between acceptable and *stay-back-away-from-my-pups* that the fox had no interest in exploring. Regardless, there was tolerance and peace in an aura about the scene, at least in the way it felt to Fen.

Rilke felt energized despite the weariness from the day's labor. He could see why people farmed. The Earth was good, had been good to Sangreave, Siena, and Florence. All of them ate canned peaches and tomato sauce; pickled beans and pickled eggs and even pickled corn. He had watched Florence put her grandmother's kraut rock gently upon the plate to press the cobs down. He had picked the cobs with his hands, pulling them down from the stalk in one swift motion. He marveled at the tassels as he shucked the corn and pulled at the threads between the kernels. It had never seemed possible to grow so many things, though his mother had gardened and cooked food that everyone raised in the parking lots near the stadium.

"Life has these happy moments too," he murmured to himself, pleased that he could be enjoying contentment after so many unhappy days in his early life. He had never been free to enjoy moments like these, yet here he was, finally feeling good about himself. He felt strangely sad that his ma so rarely had shared this kind of joy with him.

But she had done something else, and he saw then that she had loved him fiercely. He had never been hungry and she'd always make him eat before she did. Usually he was too eager to leave so he could go play with his friends, or look for things to read. So she ate what he left. But she had fed him and clothed him and sat with him when he was sick. And he knew she had loved him in her own way, and some of that was because she had been afraid of losing him.

While she watched Rilke think through these thoughts, Fen thought again about what Siena had said to her. She knew the books that Rilke had borrowed from Florence were upsetting sometimes. She put off talking with him about it. She needed to reassure him somehow, before he kept her awake all night yet again with his racing, guilty thoughts.

"You can stop worrying. I know we need to stay with Siena and Florence for the winter."

"Siena seems to think so," he said aloud, too low to hear.

"She told me so, and she explained why." Fen latched part of this truth down so that it would not be pulled upward into the cyclone of Rilke's thoughts, the slow and steady spin of feelings so intense that Fen did best to avoid them.

"What do you think?"

Fen could tell he meant the question. But she didn't answer.

"I mean, I could stay here through the winter gladly! I really enjoy the books Florence is lending me to read and I like knowing that you're safe and comfortable . . ." He trailed off the last bit of his words and shifted over to thinking, directly to Fen. "I'm afraid and I have a lot to learn. I can't keep you safe and I can't protect you like Canto could."

She had to respond, especially since this was her best chance at getting home, and she wasn't even sure if Canto was alive anyway. Besides, Canto had not come for her, which made her believe he was gone. Every day she would ask Siena the news. They would walk across the farm and think about the news together, and it was clear the only story that Fen wished to hear was that Canto had made it home safely and was down at the station to pick her up.

She'd take one last truck ride with Rilke and Siena, and she would put her face out the window the entire time. She would show up at the station and say "What's up?" to Doll as she trotted up to Canto. And there he would be, ready to take her back home. The trouble was, she couldn't remember details. Like what his face looked like. Or even how his voice sounded or how tall he was. This made getting home even more important to her. But since he hadn't found her yet, maybe she should give him more time.

As the orange hue of the setting sun filtered through the wooden slats of the barn, it cast a lattice of light and shadow over the hay-strewn floor. Rilke sat on an upturned crate, his gaze lingering on the soft bundle of puppies that tumbled around in the box. Fen, perched atop a bale of hay beside him, tilted her head in contemplation, her eyes flickering with warm amber light.

"Do you think Siena will ever want another dog?" Fen was fascinated by the energetic mass of pups and couldn't turn away from watching them. The mother had stood up and stretched after they had been there for a while. She had even touched noses with Fen and allowed Rilke to scratch her ears before walking to the corner where her food and water had been prepared for her. She wagged her tail contentedly and ate her food with gusto.

A thoughtful expression crossed Rilke's face as he watched the puppies. He hadn't considered it until now, but the idea resonated within him, sparking a hopeful warmth that spread through his chest. "You know, that idea's not half bad." Rilke said aloud, turning to face Fen.

"She'll be mourning Webb forever otherwise," Fen's fur rustled in a passing breeze.

Their shared contemplation was interrupted by the creaking of the barn door as Sangreave entered, the leathered and tired lines of his face relaxing into a grin at the sight of Rilke and his little spitz. He leaned heavily on his cane and moved quietly so he wouldn't disturb them.

"Siena's on her way." Sangreave wiped his weathered hands on a rag. "You two have done good work today. The woodpile's never looked better." He handed Rilke a stack of coins much greater than the agreed-upon amount, along with a cloth pouch.

"Thanks, Mr. Sangreave," Rilke rose to his feet. "This is too much."

Sangreave waved his hand dismissively. "You put that to good use. Eat some ice cream when you get midway on the Narrow Road. He smiled and winked. "You too, little Fen. Put some meat on your bones."

Fen looked up, panting, and wagged her tail comically. It was nice of him to finally use her name. She was pleased on

Rilke's behalf too. She knew it had bothered him.

Rilke's eyes darted briefly to the puppies before meeting the old man's smiling gaze through his thick glasses. "We enjoyed watching the pups."

Sangreave followed Rilke's glance and let out a chuckle. "They're a handful, alright. But they'll make fine dogs come Christmas time when they're old enough to leave their mama."

"Would it be possible—for Siena, I mean. As a Christmas gift. We'd work extra."

"Ah, I'd like to help you out," Sangreave said, continuing to grin from ear to ear in his well-intentioned way. "But I've already promised every one to folks around here. They've been spoken for since they were no more than a twinkle in their mama's eye."

Rilke felt the disappointment settle heavily in his stomach and was sure it was visible on his face.

"Tell you what," Sangreave added after a thoughtful pause, "I'll let you know if anything changes."

Rilke and Fen waited at the edge of the rustling cornfield. Far in the distance, Rilke thought he heard a train, but then he realized it was just the wind in the copse of trees nearby. Some crows took flight, seven that he'd been observing. They had been feasting on the remnants of corn at the edge of the field. Sangreave liked to leave a little there for the wildlife, since it kept them out of his best corn, near the house.

"Here she comes."

Rilke looked around expecting to see the truck, but Fen reminded him that she could hear things he could not. She had other sensory enhancements that were difficult to explain, she said. A few seconds later, a cloud of dust billowed from the dirt road as the old red pickup truck rumbled toward them, its engine growling tiredly through the still evening air. Siena leaned out of the open window as she brought the vehicle to a halt and gravel crunched under the tires.

"Y'all ready?" Her voice was warm but weary. She'd had her own work to do and was ready to get home for dinner.

"Yup." Rilke pulled himself into the truck's cab. Fen agilely jumped in after him, settling into the seat between Rilke and Siena. They left the farm behind, the truck's headlights carving a path through the encroaching darkness. Fen relaxed into a silvery gray and looked more like herself the further they went down the road.

"Long day?" Siena asked, casting a sidelong glance at Rilke as they bumped along the road.

"A good day," he said, turning to watch the hills darken in the diminishing light.

Once home, Siena disappeared outside again to clean out the back of the truck and secure the garage. Florence was waiting for them, her presence framed in the doorway.

"Evening, you two," Florence called out, her gaze softening at the sight of them. "How was the farm?"

"Good," Rilke answered as he followed Fen inside, and looked to make sure Siena was still in the garage. He lowered his voice. "Sangreave's dog had pups."

"Really?" Interest sparked in Florence's eyes. "I bet they're adorable."

"They are," Rilke agreed, taking a seat at the table. "Fen and I thought maybe one would make a good friend for Siena."

Fen leaped gracefully onto a chair, her tail swishing. "She's in a loop of grief. I feel it everywhere," the fox added, before finding some cornbread set aside for her on a plate and snapping it up. Florence had even poured some buttermilk over it, and Fen lapped up the last bit, savoring every soggy crumb.

"Losing Webb hit her hard. She tries to hide it." Florence sat down as well and rested her chin on the heel of her hand.

"Problem is, Sangreave's promised them all away," Rilke added as he recalled the disappointment. "Would have been nice though, right?"

"Would have." Florence traced the grain of the table with her fingers. "But it's the thought that counts. You two always have good intentions."

Rilke's thoughts drifted back to the puppies. Fen padded over, her paws soft on the stone floor. Though cybernetic implants allowed her to communicate, she was still more animal than either of them. She had also been excited about the possibility of a puppy around the house to play with and chase. Someone shorter, at eye level.

Fen nudged Rilke's hand affectionately. It would be good for him too. He needed privacy for the new thoughts his reading brought him every day. He needed to talk about these ideas with other people, to learn how to be a human being. And he needed to learn how to listen to an animal without the augmentations Fen had. Otherwise, when Canto came to retrieve her, wouldn't Rilke be lonely?

The evening light drained from the room, leaving shadows to play upon the walls. Rilke leaned back in his chair at the dining table, feeling the weight of the day's labor settle into his bones. He imagined the soft, sleepy bundles of fur nestled against each other in Sangreave's barn. Fen's presence was a silent comfort at his side, their minds temporarily in different places, without each other.

"Could you pass the salt?" Siena's voice cut through his

reverie, her hand outstretched across the table.

"Sure," Rilke replied automatically, sliding the shaker down the worn wooden surface. Siena had been too busy all day to stop and eat so she was having some fried potatoes. Florence and Rilke were having their nightly kettle of peppermint tea.

The ring of the phone sounded from Siena's office. Florence disappeared into the other room to answer the call, her steps soft but deliberate.

"Maybe it's about that rare book she's been hunting for her archive," Siena muttered.

"Or someone with an old vinyl collection to donate," Rilke added.

Fen's thoughts shimmered hopefully in Rilke's mind.

Seconds ticked by, punctuated by the clink of Siena's fork on her plate. Rilke's thoughts strayed to the barn, the puppies, and the ineluctable pull of something they couldn't have.

Florence re-entered the room, a curious lilt to her step that caught everyone's attention immediately. The phone was still cradled between her ear and shoulder as she smiled, surprise dancing in her eyes.

"It's for you."

Rilke stood up, exchanging a puzzled look with Fen, whose eyes flickered. They moved together to where Florence held out the receiver. In the other room, Siena grumbled about dinner being a lonely affair, what with everyone having left her alone. But then she helped herself to some more potatoes and was quiet again salting her food and pouring a glass of cold water from the carafe.

"Hello?"

"Kid," came the gravelly voice of Sangreave, warm and jovial. "Been thinking about our talk today. I reckon I can part with one after all, come December, when they're old enough. Got to talking with the missus, and we decided that yellow one with the patch of white on its belly would be better off with you folks."

"Truly?" Rilke gripped the phone tighter, hope and elation blossoming within him. Beside him, Fen's tail swished eagerly.

"You bet," Sangreave chuckled. "I'll bring the pup by on Christmas Eve. And no more talk of money. Life's a gift."

"Thank you, Mr. Sangreave," Rilke breathed out, gratitude swelling in his chest.

"Think nothing of it. Just make sure Siena takes good care of him."

"We will. I promise." Rilke's hand trembled slightly as he handed the phone back to Florence, who ended the call with polite farewells.

"Can you believe it?" Rilke turned to Fen, his smile reflecting the fox's excitement. A surge of shared joy transmitted between them.

It was Christmas Eve, and everyone had crowded around the tree to enjoy the evening. They had all eaten well. Rilke and Fen were waiting for the sign from Florence. The phone rang, and in a minute or two, Florence nodded to Rilke. He in turn made up some excuse for walking outside in the December rain and wind to meet Sangreave at the end of the drive. It was a steep walk, but his excitement over the new addition kept him focused and positive despite the weather.

"You got him?" Sangreave was on the passenger side of the car as he handed the small whining box to Rilke. There was a nod to Sangreave's son, home from service in Maine for the holidays, then the two of them backed out into the empty road and pulled away, leaving Rilke holding the box that tipped in his hands as the pup circled around inside. It was a big box and the pup felt much heavier than the one Rilke and Fen had seen a month before.

Rilke carefully and quickly made his way back to the house, coming in a side gate to the courtyard and then into Florence's tower, where she waited with a warm blanket and a bow. Fen stood eagerly by, watching as the puppy, larger than before, was brought out of the box to Florence's waiting arms. The pup had bright brown eyes and a wiggly butt. His tail was flying back and forth and he panted and wriggled in Florence's arms before leaning back to lick her face while Florence winced and laughed.

Quickly, she wrapped the blanket around the squirming pup and wiped her mouth with her arm. Rilke tied the bow gently while the playful puppy tried to fight him.

"Ow! His teeth are like needles!" Rilke remarked after finishing the bow. For a second the pup strained his head side to side trying to untie it before Florence distracted him with singing and cuddled him to her. "There, you rascal!" she chided, and the three of them headed for the lodge where Siena waited.

Fen knew that the puppy would find Siena's heart in the most direct way possible. Initially, she had wanted to redeem herself in Siena's eyes, but that original desire rapidly gave way to a stronger wish to see her happy again, the way she had been in Webb's memories. Siena had been kind to Rilke and Fen, allowing them both to stay as guests in her house, and even though they had worked for her, Florence, and Sangreave over the past two months, the work had been light and cheerful.

When Siena saw the puppy, her first word was "No," but that negative fell apart as she looked at the large paws, the lolling tongue, and the bright inquisitive eyes. She saw something there. Perhaps it was the way the little fella began to gallop toward her after Florence let him down to the floor, but tripped and tumbled over his feet. Or the way she already had a vision of this dog, grown, walking the fence line with her the way Webb used to.

Florence smiled at Siena's happiness. Siena caught her look and beamed back. There was something about a puppy that made Siena seem ten years younger. Finally, the scales had fallen from Siena's heart, and everyone watched the transformation in awe. Overnight, Siena even started talking differently to Fen, asking for the fox's help directly. She didn't try to hide her curiosity and asked Fen all kinds of questions about the temperature in the room and the softness of a new bed that she had pulled together made from scraps of alpaca wool and her old shirts.

For days, it seemed the three of them were together constantly. Sometimes the puppy slept curled up next to Fen in the new pillowy bed by the window, and at other times, he slept between Fen and Siena on the couch, on his back, feet in the air. Everyone was happier, more optimistic, even when January brought ice instead of rain and 2150 opened with a wind storm that damaged an area of the windowed hallway near the exterior door. A tree had come down and they kept that part of the house shut against the pup's wandering. But every obstacle seemed surmountable with the addition of the pup.

When mid-January brought unseasonable temperatures in the single digits, the pup brightened the quiet of the house with his zest for chasing and being chased by the ecstatic Fen. The quarreling chitter of the fox's play sent Florence into hysterics and she and Rilke often held their stomachs because they laughed so hard. Siena couldn't help but admire how fast the fox moved to evade the pup's sharp-toothed grip.

"Are you going to name him? It's been almost a month, Siena." Florence was washing dishes one night while Fen played tug-of-war gently with a rope knot and the littlest member of the house.

"I was thinking 'Dog,'" Siena murmured with deadpan seriousness.

"How about 'Griffin,' since he seems to fly when he runs. You can call him 'Grif,' or 'Griffin O'Malley Brimburner' when he's in trouble." Rilke had been speed-reading through a set of linked young adult novels from when Florence was a girl, and the character's name did seem like a good fit for the speedy pup.

Siena looked up, taking the name seriously. Already he appeared to be like Webb, not fully hound or retriever, but fast, with an excellent nose for coursing and finding. He was smart, too.

"Okay, that's pretty good," Siena said.

Fen looked up. "How about Poopy Face."

The pup growled at her and barked.

Fen pulled her head back, arching her neck, and looked down at him. "Oh, oh? You want to take me? You gotta catch me first!"

Then she darted out of the kitchen. To heighten the game, she had made herself match the surfaces of everything around her, rendering herself all but invisible. This was the puppy's favorite game since he had to be fast and find her by scent alone. He was able to do this with alarming ease, though Siena still found it disconcerting when the fox applied her camouflaging abilities to playtime. It didn't seem right that any animal should be able to do that. But then again, knowing that Fen could conceal herself made Siena more hopeful for the trip that lay ahead for both the fox and Rilke.

What an advantage, and hopefully something they wouldn't have to rely on too much. She shook the thought away and instead watched as a shimmery, reflective form trotted through the kitchen relaxedly.

"Where's Grif?" Siena asked, feeling the rightness of the name as she said it.

Fen sat back, just a silhouette of fox along the edges. "He caught me. So it's his turn to hide."

Siena nodded. "You going to go find him? I'm sure he's hidden by now."

"Nah," said Fen, "I want to see how long it takes for him to figure it out." Then she gave her chittering laugh and disappeared through the dog door to the outside courtyard.

Dodie and the Snowbird

February drew winter out and they all felt the strain of being stuck in the house most days. The winter had been unusually hard, with first a downed tree on the windowed corridor and now the truck not starting. Siena was headed down to Sangreave's to take his wife some soup that Florence had made and the engine would not turn over. She sat in the garage, and placed her head on the steering wheel in defeat. "Damn." This was not going to be an easy fix, and they'd have to simply wait out the winter until she could call for a mechanic. Then they'd have to order the part. It would be weeks.

When Siena returned after just a few minutes, soup still in her arms, Florence had a feeling.

"Oh, baby. I'm so sorry." Siena set the soup down and they fell into a long embrace. Even though a head shorter, Florence's hugs made her seem like the larger presence, as warm and loving as it was.

"I just can't give it up," she said, realizing that she was on the verge. It wasn't practical any more. Maybe it was time to retire the truck.

There was yet another surprise the winter would bring them. The old solar panels that Siena had gotten for free from a neighbor twelve years before began to not hold a charge. As the cold weather dipped and stayed lower earlier and longer, this caused freezing and cracking in the battery case. Fortunately, there was a backup wood stove for heating and cooking in the lodge, so at night everyone stayed near the fire and its comforting warmth until time to head up to bed. Siena also managed to get the old biomass boiler going so that other parts of the house could be warm, but they had just enough pellets for two weeks of heat, and without the truck, no one was going anywhere.

Without electricity, they talked more. Florence played her ukulele and they sang songs or told stories. It was Valentine's Day and Florence had insisted that they bring out the chocolate elixir that someone had sent them as a gift. It was synthetic, the wholesale trade of cocoa ended when international labor laws and climate change caught up to one another. Fortunately, there was always a solution provided by science.

"Which one should we try?" Siena held up a bag with a Mayan design and another with a picture of a mountain and something in French.

"Let's try the Swiss," Florence suggested, preparing the stove. She brought mugs down from the shelf and poured in hot water from the kettle to warm them. She worked at the stove for a while and everyone else readied the house for the night. Siena and Fen took Grif outside and they were back in a flash. Both canids did a shimmy in front of the door to rid themselves of snow.

"Whew! It is COLD out there. And still snowing." Siena hung her hat and coat up near the courtyard door and toweled Grif quickly while he wiggled and writhed. The pup tore through the house with excitement, glad to be inside again. Siena also dried Fen who was more subdued than Grif, but grateful. She pounced away looking for the pup and eager to get cozy by the fire. Siena then brought some logs from the porch box and set them near the stove. After checking to be sure it was roaring, she shut the latch and returned the poker to its holder.

Rilke was already on the couch nearest the stove, close by a solar lamp and reading. Florence tousled his curls and told him he was going to hurt his eyesight reading in the dark. He passed the book to her and she put it aside as she handed him a steaming mug. Siena settled on the couch and Florence came back with two more mugs in hand.

"My grandmother used to tell stories to help me learn, but also to fall asleep," said Siena, as she made room on the couch for Florence.

"What kind of stories?" Rilke felt warm by the stove and pulled the blanket around his legs.

"There was one I always loved to hear her tell whenever she was trying to get me to settle down in the evenings, especially when I had been rowdy or hard to manage." Siena accepted the mug from Florence, who snorted with laughter.

"You? Difficult? Never," said Florence as she sat down beside Siena with her own mug. Siena squeezed Florence's knee and kissed her lightly on the cheek.

"She just can't stand having to be quiet while I tell a story for a change," Siena said to Rilke while glancing over at Florence. Then she continued on.

"My favorite story was 'Dodie and the Snowbird.'"

Florence nodded. "I like this too. It's a classic." The elixir was good and rich, and Florence leaned back against Siena who put her arm around her and pulled her close.

"My Momaw Willie said her Great-Great-Momaw Dollie told this story first, so it originated with her in the mid-1900s."

Rilke took a sip from his mug and found it miraculous. Fen padded into the room just then, puppy in tow, and jumped onto the couch beside Rilke. The puppy whined, looking pitifully up at Fen, who stuck her tongue out slightly before circling into Rilke's side.

"Come here, you," Siena scooped Grif up into her arms and helped him find a place to nestle against Florence. Once everyone was comfortable, she began the story, and the evening took on the glow of memory, and deeper memory still.

Dodie lived in the woods with her brother, Jimmie. Usually they played well together, but one afternoon Jimmie was being especially mischievous and did a number of things that upset Dodie. They were the sort of things little brothers do that big sisters find annoying, like leave toys lying around without picking them up and spilling juice all over the table where the dolls and stuffed animals were taking tea, and—

"Seriously? 'Taking tea?' Who even does that?" Florence chortled, and Siena playfully pretend-slapped her leg.

"I'm telling the story, not you," she said, and began again.

By late afternoon, Dodie's patience wore out. She pinched Jimmie really hard when he wouldn't stop kicking her chair while she was trying to read. He let out a howl and Dodie's mother came into the room to see what the matter was.

"Dodie pinched me!" yelled Jimmie, and Dodie realized that once again, she was in trouble, and it wasn't even her fault.

"Why do I always get in trouble when he's the one causing the problem!" she screamed back at her mom. Keep in mind, Dodie had been babysitting since breakfast, without a break. At least, that's the way she felt about it.

Dodie and Jimmie's mother was tired most of all. She had been washing dishes and clothes all day—

"What do you mean she was washing clothes and dishes all day? Didn't she have a butler? Or a domestic machine?" Fen's questions broke loudly into Siena's mind and she stopped for a moment, wondering how to explain what the twentieth century might have been like to a cybernetic fox two centuries later.

The truth was, Siena hadn't thought about it much herself. When she was young, the state offered automated domestic support to anyone who had a child. But the woman in this story had two children and still had to wash her clothes by hand and mop the floors. Siena understood that Florence just enjoyed the feel of warm water on her hands and the peacefulness of "washing the dishes to wash the dishes," as she would always say, quoting some Buddhist philosopher from the 1990s. But washing clothes by hand said something else entirely about this woman and her children, and maybe Siena hadn't thought about it enough.

It had been a long time since anyone but Siena had told the story and that was also on her mind this time of year. She always missed her Momaw Willie in late winter. The mountains always felt lonely, but especially when the snow had covered everything unexpectedly, and the birds had crept into dark sheltering spaces that a human could not know about.

"This was long before Grif, Rilke, Florence, and Fen." Her voice softened as she looked each of them in the eye when saying their names, concluding with the fox and a long gentle stare.

"In fact, during this time, memory died with each person, unless they had told someone a story. A story was the only way to remember how things had been. There were no projections, screens, or pins that made it possible for foxes to speak. Animals and humans could not communicate with one another as you and I do, and the whole world was silent and lonely, and life was hard. They didn't even know about the cycle of the oceans, or how many people would still remember life as they had lived it two hundred years later. They still thought they had plenty of time."

Fen shivered and tucked herself into Rilke and drifted on the words of Siena as she began yet again.

A long, long time ago, before you and me, Dodie lived at the edge of a deep, dark wood with her little brother, Jimmie, and her mother. Because their mother took in wash for the neighbors, she often had extra work to do and less time for tending to her children. So Dodie ended up, more often than not, the caretaker of her brother.

He was a hard kid to play with, because he constantly needed attention, and Dodie's attention wasn't enough. Dodie often felt put aside by her mother, even though she was strong and could work too. Why did she have to constantly watch after Jimmie? He sometimes got her into trouble and it was all so that their mother would stop her work (washing and tending and cleaning and cooking and mending) in order to love him, and to show that love by chastising Dodie and ordering her to keep him happy.

Dodie would sigh and make more of an effort to play with Jimmie, because he was barely three and the only little brother she had. He didn't really want to get her in trouble. He just missed their mother too. Keep in mind, this is long before women began to receive reparations for the labor lost by previous generations. No, Dodie's mother did everything by hand, including grow the food, preserve the food, and make the money to buy the food . . .

Florence interrupted in exactly the place Sienna expected.

"So we're going to hear the seventh wave of feminism version now, are we?"

Siena huffed and made a motion as if she were going to stand up. But she was off balance, her back seized up unexpectedly, and the hot mug of elixir in her hand went flying.

The bizarre element everyone thought about afterwards was how they each expected the mug to spill and could even imagine that it had already happened in slow motion. But the truth was far more unsettling. Faster than anyone could see, Fen leaped from her place at the end of the couch, capturing the mug and its contents in one seamless movement. Everyone noted the extended hand of Siena and her alarmed expression. In the next two seconds, she had sunk back into her seat with a pained grimace on her face, clutching her back, and the mug sat serenely on the table before her. Fen was close, head tilted, looking expectantly and intensely at Siena, who readjusted herself and insisted that her back was fine. The spasm had surprised her, but not as much as the fox's unnatural reflex.

No one said anything at first, but then they all heard the frustrated and ringing voice of Fen in their minds. Even Grif had stopped chewing his toy and was watching the scene with attention, one little tooth poking up over his lip in an underbite and one ear flipped backwards over his crown.

"Tell the story the way Momaw Willie told it." Fen insisted firmly and somewhat impatiently. There was a zeal for exactitude in the fox's expression that no one challenged, though later it might have seemed out of place in that wonder that they all had felt in the presence of her acrobatic recovery of the falling mug.

This is the story Siena told until its end, without further interruptions.

Once upon a time, quite a long time ago in fact, there lived a young girl named Dodie. She lived with her brother in a forest. Sometimes Dodie had to watch her brother while their mother worked, running the house and taking in washing for the neighbors. And sometimes, little Jimmie picked fights with his sister until their mother came to scold them.

Dodie always felt like her mother was unfair. One day in particular, when Jimmie had been unusually mischievous, and their mother was especially tired and frustrated, Dodie broke into sobs.

"You always take his side!" She fled into the yard and screamed "I hate you!" back at the house before running into the woods.

She didn't stop. She ran and she ran until she was out of breath. She ran past the only path she knew and onto another she didn't. She ran along through the pines until she had to stop and put her hands on her knees and catch her breath.

At this point, she wasn't sure where the path went. She had never been this far away from the house alone. She started walking in the direction she thought her house should be, but when the pines gave way to bramble, she turned and walked another way. Each time she turned, she tried a different path, but the trees all looked alike and it was getting darker.

The sky wasn't just dark because the afternoon was getting late, but because a storm was coming. She hadn't noticed before, but a low rumble confirmed her worst fear. There were little rain drops that turned into much larger raindrops.

As if on cue, lightning streaked quietly across the sky and she heard the rumble again, this time much closer. The rain began to come down so hard that it hurt her arms.

Frantic, Dodie began to run, this time toward the largest tree she could find. But the lightning found it first and a bright burst of light and fire nearly blinded her. The tree exploded into burnt bark and hot sap. Though it did not catch fire in the pelting rain, the force and the jolt made her hair stand on end and sent a shiver up through her feet and out her fingers.

She screamed and ran, this time away from the tree, and toward a bluff concealed by a row of mountain laurel. With a startled shriek, she tumbled into the scrubby trees and twisted her ankle. Down, down she went, rolling along a steep embankment that gave way in sharp pieces of slate under her feet. She kept sliding and feeling the rip of her clothes, as twigs tangled in her hair. When she finally stopped rolling, she lay at the bottom. She was sobbing, cut, and bleeding with bruises and scrapes from head to toe. She even tasted blood in her mouth, from having bust her lip on a rock.

She was scared, injured, and worst of all—exposed in a lightning storm. As another crackling fork of electricity spread across the sky, the hail began to fall, tiny pieces of ice like marbles that hurt each time they hit. Covering her head, Dodie dragged herself toward a tree root that had been upturned along the embankment. While the storm raged around her, she huddled into a small alcove, sheltered by the root of the tree. There, she cried herself to sleep.

Dodie awoke to the feeling of being watched. Two squirrels stood on a branch in the moonlight looking down at her. They seemed curious, and now and then one would scurry to the left and right. When she sat up, they both made a screeching sound and scurried away briskly.

The storm had passed, leaving occasional distant grumbles in its wake. The moon was bright in the newly clear night sky. Here and there, large, puffy clouds drifted by, illuminated by the moon which was brighter than anything Dodie had ever seen. But then another cloud began to gather overhead until the moon was once again cloaked in darkness. Dodie began to cry, quietly at first, then more loudly as she broke into sobs. Her belly hurt from the weeping. Or was she hungry? She deeply regretted running away and she even missed Jimmie, but especially her mother. As tears streaked down her dirty cheeks, she burrowed her face in her knees and hugged them tighter.

"Don't cry," said a warm voice near her. Just then, the moon spread its light across the indigo sky and the clouds were glowing again in the reflected light. A giant alabaster bird stood in front of her, easily two times the height of Dodie, and even taller than her mother. The bird had a kind expression, and tilted her crested head to the side in wonderment.

"Why are you crying, Dodie? The storm has passed."

"How do you know my name?"

"I know many things. I know that you do not always get along with your brother."

Dodie looked down when the snowbird said this.

"I wish I hadn't run away."

The snowbird looked a little sad then bopped her head to the side jauntily.

"You must be hungry. Climb on my back and we'll go somewhere so that you can warm up." Dodie didn't feel the cold anymore, but she was excited to reach up into the feathery ruff of the giant bird and feel how soft it was. The snowbird extended her wing and Dodie was able to climb up. There was a petite, blue padded seat with stirrups. They were a perfect fit, just the right length.

"Hold on!" said the snowbird, then she hopped twice before beating her wings, once, twice, and again in great ponderous thumps. These escalated into a lift that Dodie had never imagined possible. She held on tight to the seat's handles which were engraved in delicate gold and silver filigree.

As they rose into the air and steadily advanced higher aloft, the snow began to fall. But this didn't matter to Dodie who watched the landscape shrink below her then disappear completely.

They entered the first of many cloud layers. If the clouds had been lit by the moon before, they seemed as if they were the true illumination in the sky now. The silver orb of the moon was smaller now than it had been. In every direction as Dodie looked, the sky took on the quality of a snowy quilt with a crisp, azure sky stretching on forever. But then changed to a landscape of white sand, the moon a tiny pearl so far away, and becoming further away every second, even though it seemed sometimes like they flew toward it. The moon kept drifting farther away, becoming smaller until it disappeared completely. Then finally, as if an island in a sea of air, another cloud appeared and into it they drifted until it could have been day or it might have been night, so confused was Dodie's sense of time.

They came to another land where there were trees like there were back home, but it was summer and the air was warm. Gone were the fears of the night before. Had it been the night before? Or much longer? She wasn't sure. She didn't care.

Below her, the land was swept with joy and light as if a great painter had waved a brush across it and beauty had spiraled over everything. The invisible tint of the brush was a spectrum that only a god could see. The edges were distinct and perfect at every focus. Dodie had the thought she might be dreaming. But no, it was real, and she knew that it was real in a way she herself had never felt before.

The snowbird circled to land and Dodie held tightly as the bird hopped to a halt. She stretched her wing forth once more so Dodie could climb down.

When Dodie slid down the silvery wing, she landed on soft green grass, but her feet were bare. She thought this odd, but the feeling was so grand she burst into a laugh and looked at the snowbird with delight.

"Come with me," the snowbird said with a coolness that felt different from the glade around them, from the swaying trees, the flowers, the bees as they danced from flower to flower. Dodie thought it might be like home except animals were lounging about as if they were friends. When they saw Dodie, there was a general flurry of excitement and they began to approach her. At first she was afraid, but the snowbird brought her closer under the shade of her wing.

"They won't harm you. They are just curious." There were animals Dodie had never seen before, but each one was gentle. They spoke to her kindly and she understood them.

"Who are you?" asked a red dog with long hair.

"Where did you get those flat feet?" a deer nosed into the

circle around Dodie.

"You're pretty," said a calico cat as she rubbed against Dodie's leg.

"Give her some space, everyone." The snowbird walked with Dodie to a small knoll where a picnic basket sat atop a soft blanket. A tree was lit with green light as the sun streamed through the leaves and made the time feel like an endless afternoon.

In the picnic basket was a feast of Dodie's favorite foods. She ate quickly, trying to be polite, but far hungrier than she had realized before. Afterward, she lay back on the blanket and rested her head on the snowbird's light-warmed wing. Just as she was barefoot, so too she wore a comfortable long dress of soft cotton, a pale green like the mosses against her skin, with delicate embroidered flowers on the sleeve and collar. Her scrapes were gone, as was the blood that had initially crusted uncomfortably on her arms. But she was clean and felt warm and full all at once. A gray tabby curled up alongside her as she rested with the snowbird, and he made biscuits with his paws in her side.

A spotted puppy with long black ears found a place too, near Dodie's feet. A speckled pony grazed nearby, and would occasionally study Dodie, a single blade of grass hanging from his mouth as he chewed lazily. Bucking goats capered along the hillside. Little pink piglets chased one another in the grass. A brown cow and her calf lazed in the sun. The mama rolled her head around to her young and gave him a generous lick as he stood up and wobbled. Then he fell back down in the buttercups beside her.

Dodie felt at peace, but her memory was a bit hazy whenever she tried to recall how she had gotten here. There had been a storm, perhaps she had been lost, but everything else was fading. She didn't care. It was so nice here in the sun, with the giant bird beside her in the soft grass.

"Are you happy here?" The snowbird seemed sadder as they lay in the sun. She had been particularly quiet while Dodie finished eating. Looking back to where the basket had been, Dodie saw that it had disappeared. This place was unusual, but Dodie wanted to stay forever. The cat was purring relaxedly beside her. Two lambs pounced near the calf who began to join in the fun, and the three of them frolicked while Dodie watched.

"You don't miss your mother and little Jimmie?" The snowbird shifted and Dodie sat up. Yes. That was his name. Jimmie. She remembered his grubby face and his silly ideas. He could be funny sometimes. He could make her laugh when no one else could. And her mother. She worked so hard to take care of her and Jimmie. When Dodie thought of her mother, she also remembered the angry words which she had shouted toward the house when she had run away. She didn't hate her mother, could never hate her mother. She hadn't meant it, and longed to be with her mother now, to tell her how much she loved her and how sorry she was for running away. Dodie patted the cat and scratched the ears of the puppy that had snuggled against her, then carefully stood up.

"I have really enjoyed being here, but I need to get home. My mother will be so worried." As Dodie said this, more of her memory came back to her of the storm and how frightened she had been. She knew her mother would be upset and looking everywhere for her. The snowbird stretched her wings broadly in the sun, and beat them softly in preparation for the flight ahead. She didn't say anything more, but stretched her wing for Dodie and waited as the child settled her feet in the stirrups. Around them, the animals gathered, some nibbling on the saddle or Dodie's toes affectionately, and others telling her how much they enjoyed her company.

"Come back, Dodie! We would love to see you again!" said the lambs.

"We'll miss you!" said the cat as he emerged from between the heifer's hooves.

"You are always welcome here, friend," bayed the hound. A tiny fox kit poked its nose out from its mother's brush. A turkey with her poults milled about, mingling with some ducklings that had waddled up from the nearby pond. Everywhere, as many animals as Dodie had ever imagined or knew about had come to say goodbye.

As the snowbird began her run and the *whomp, whomp, whomp* of her gigantic wings pushed the air away, they lifted up again. Dodie waved at the animals and watched as they grew fainter in the distance. Up they went into a tiny cloud that became a larger cloud, and finally yet another cloud layer. The sky was once again like a field of blue, this time brighter, but she could see the small orb of the moon in the daytime sky far in the distance. They climbed at first into cloud layers that may have been like smooth white fields and others like billowy mountains, but eventually they began to descend again and the weather was cold and rainy. Dodie took a deep breath as the rain stung her arms and legs.

She looked down and saw that her clothes were badly ripped. The knees were torn in her dungarees and she was missing a shoe. Everywhere, blood had dried on little wounds that had reddened and were feeling itchy in the wet air. The rain formed pink rivulets along her arms and legs as she and the bird were drenched by torrents of heavy raindrops.

The bird brought her feet forward and the two of them softly landed in the clearing near Dodie's house. She knew where she was and could get home from here. Sore, and feeling the bruises of her fall from the night before, Dodie took her time finding the ground. She looked up into the kindly face of the snowbird and then threw her arms around her neck. They stood that way for a while, and when Dodie pulled back to look her in the face, the snowbird let fall a tear, perfectly round and iridescent.

Dodie caught the tear and noticed it looked exactly like a pearl. She looked back at the bird who stood tall again, and raised her plumed crest with excitement.

"You are home now, and your mother is eager to see you. Jimmie too." The bird wasn't sad now, but there was still a slight melancholy to her voice that Dodie understood. She felt it too. She would miss the bird and the animals, the golden afternoon above the clouds.

"Would you stay here for just a minute? I want my mother and brother to meet you! They'll never believe me otherwise." The bird carefully nodded once, then stepped backward from Dodie as the child ran from the pine-thick glen to the nearby house, shouting "I'm back! Mom! Jimmie! I'm home!"

Dodie was barely into the back yard before her mother, tear-streaked and wearing her Sunday dress, ran to meet her. She was sobbing and was nearly incapable of speech as she pulled Dodie to her and squeezed her in a tight embrace. Then Jimmie ran into the yard, also crying, as did several of their neighbors and other people she knew from church.

Dodie tried to tell her mother about the snowbird and even led her and Jimmie up to the glen where she expected the large bird to be waiting, but there was no one there. Not a feather, not a sign that there had been a massive bird with a velvet saddle or that Dodie had flown to another world and had a picnic with talking animals. As she tried to tell her mother, Dodie realized how it all sounded. Her mother kept touching her face and crying, then pulling her towards her saying, "I know, honey. It's alright. Everything is fine now."

Only Jimmie believed her, and his face opened with wonder and delight the more she told him of what she had seen and where she had been. He hugged her too and looked up. "I believe you, Dodie!"

Later Dodie learned that everyone was there because she had been missing for several days. Searchers had given up and had begun to help others clean up after the storm, which had caused flooding in the mountain's hollows. People everywhere had lost livestock and fences, corn cribs and chickens. Dodie's absence had hit everyone hard though, and after the doctor cleared her of any major breaks, he looked at her sternly and said she was lucky to be alive after the fall she took.

No one could understand how a little girl had survived for so long in the mountains alone, but some people speculated that she had hit her head and slept for days in a fever. She kept talking about a giant bird, insisting that she had traveled up into the clouds where there were talking animals.

"How absurd!" said the pastor.

"What a vivid imagination!" said the teacher.

"Please don't run away again," pleaded her mother.

In those first moments home, Dodie heard many opinions about what she had experienced. Once she accepted that the snowbird was gone, she did wonder for a moment if it had all been just a dream.

Dodie smiled at her brother.

"I believe you," he said again, as he reached his hand toward hers. Just then, she felt something in her hand, and opened her closed fist.

In her palm lay a tiny pearl where the tear of the snowbird had fallen. It was like a moon in miniature, perfect and round.

After the story, everyone was quiet and thoughtful. Fen had the most questions.

"Where did they go?" she asked Siena. "Did they travel into the future where animals could talk?"

"I don't know," said Siena calmly.

"Was it heaven? For animals?" asked Florence.

Rilke had a similar question.

"Was it a dream? Or had she died? My uncle said sometimes children might be sick and on the edge of death for a long time. They play with other spirits while they decide to live or not."

"I don't know. My momaw never knew either. I think it's just something we have to accept on faith."

"Are you saying this actually happened?" Fen looked incredulous and Siena smiled awkwardly, squinching up one side of her face. For an animal with computerized implants, the fox seemed considerably less logical than Siena would have guessed.

"Are you saying that you find this story remotely plausible?" Siena leaned forward and focused on the fox. Fen sat up and leaned back for a moment, processing the question.

"Why would you tell a story that wasn't? Especially when we are led to believe that it was real. There was the evidence of the pearl in her pocket. That's physical proof." Fen looked smug, as if she had solved a riddle that no one else had gotten to the bottom of. Seeing where this was headed, Florence intervened.

"Maybe it's meant to be taken figuratively, like an

allegory," suggested Florence. "You know, like one of those fables meant to teach a moral. There's talking animals in those stories and they've been around for nearly three thousand years."

"A fable?" inquired Fen.

"Aesop's Fables." Florence was surprised. "I'll be right back." She grabbed her flashlight and headed toward her tower, presumably to find a book. Siena and Rilke cleaned up, rinsing the mugs in the cold water from the tap. Without electricity, they were making do, but the work didn't last long before the water stopped coming out of the spigot.

"Damn." Siena bumped her head on the cabinet and threw the hand towel down. "Guess I'll just add that to the list, then." She wearily sat back down on the couch after feeding some more wood to the stove. At least they were inside, warm, and toasty. There was water set aside for emergencies like this, but the inconvenience still made itself felt.

Florence came back to the lodge with a stack of books.

"Hon, water's frozen."

"Nothing to be done, I guess." Florence sat down on the couch and a curious Fen trotted over. There was an odd device with a rubbery pad that was torn in a couple of places and dented.

"What's that?" Fen asked.

"An encyclopedia and several other books I thought you might like. It's accessed through touch. Here, you try." Florence held out her hand to Fen, who responded in kind. Then Florence placed Fen's paw on the pad and the light started to blink faster.

"Do you hear it?"

Fen nodded as a voice whirred inside her head. She could speed up the information as she liked, and with little effort, steer the navigational menu.

"I figured you could access it. We used to have headsets at the library for people needing external aids. Some of the kids had pins and could access it the way you are now."

Fen looked at her, eyes wide and ears flicking back and forth. She continued to have the appearance of someone listening. Then she removed her paw.

"It's like a network!" Florence showed what else she had carried down from her library. She had two or three books on Aesop, and one on fables and oral literature. The books were works of art, with ornate images of animals and people throughout. Several of the stories had foxes in them, which excited Fen.

"Aesop was a Greek slave and story teller who lived a long, long time ago. Some of his stories are quite old, and many stories have been attributed to him, even some that came from other cultures." Florence flipped through and came to a page with an illustration of a donkey being carried upside down by a man and a child. "Here—this story is one of my favorites."

Florence began to read "The Miller, His Son, and the Ass" aloud and everyone listened to the story about a donkey being taken to market. The man and his son encountered different groups of people who criticized their methods, because in each case, one or both of them were riding the donkey. Finally, they ended up carrying the animal between them, but the donkey fought against the ropes as they crossed a bridge, and he fell into the river. Florence concluded the story and had to restrain herself from giggling at the very end, when the miller had given up and was headed home.

"By trying to please everybody, he had pleased nobody, and lost his Ass besides." Siena sputtered into laughter, badly held back, and Rilke caught the humor too. Florence finished with the moral, "*If you try to please all, you please none.*"

"I don't think it's funny that the ass died. Why are you all laughing?" Fen was serious, and by now Siena was holding her gut, in tears at the low brow pun. Florence stopped with a light chuckle and stroked Fen's head. The fox was alert and listening.

"Sugarfoot, it's just a story. It didn't happen. It's meant to teach a lesson through memorable characters. In this story, the miller and his son shouldn't have given a second thought to what the people around them were saying. They cared too much about what others thought, instead of doing what they believed should be done. By trying to please everyone else, they lost the one thing of value that they had."

Fen looked around the room with something like disappointment. "The donkey fell in the river and drowned. I don't see why that's funny." Fen looked at Siena who looked at Florence who looked at Rilke.

"Honey," Florence began again, "you're taking the story too seriously. We're laughing about the word, 'ass,' because it can mean a donkey, but it can also mean your butt or even your money. It's a figure of speech. It creates an image and that helps make stories fun and meaningful." Florence realized the fox wasn't convinced.

"Maybe you should read a few more of these stories, and you'll see what I mean." Florence tapped her finger on the info pad. "They are meant to make people think, and the animals make the stories interesting for children. But we aren't supposed to take them literally. The talking animals establish that it's a fantasy."

"But I'm talking to you now." Fen was beginning to sound indignant, which was an unexpected turn for the evening to take. Even Rilke looked up from his reading. Florence was thinking carefully about what her next words were. Siena looked like she wanted to stay out of the discussion, but was listening intently, ready to see what would happen next. Only the puppy was indifferent, snoring with his feet up in the air.

"Fen," Florence began, "these stories were composed long ago, hundreds, even thousands of years. Animals didn't talk. And—" she seemed about to say something but stopped, reconsidering. It was too late. Fen had heard the thought which had moved faster than words ever could. Without intending to, Florence was acknowledging the obvious but difficult fact that stories about animals were easier for humans to take a lesson from, especially when animals died or were eaten by other animals because they made bad choices. It was there, unspoken, but hanging in the air nonetheless.

"I'm going up to my room," Fen announced loudly in the minds of everyone except the pup. She walked over, checked to make sure Grif was warm and sleeping comfortably, then faced the others.

"I'm going to read every story in here about a fox. I saw the pictures. I know there are several." Fen took the info pad gently into her mouth, and walked out of the room solemnly, as if she had been handed a difficult responsibility.

Fen would make up her own mind about what the stories taught, and if the lessons could be trusted. Most of all, she wanted to see what so many years of human civilization had to say about foxes. It would help her understand how she was seen by the human beings around her, and also the ones who created her and gave her a mind.

After Fen left the room, she headed for a quiet place. She needed to read and to think.

Siena was the first to say anything. "I don't think my momaw ever thought anyone would be telling that story to a real talking animal."

Florence looked briefly at the table of contents in a book of Aesop's fables with vivid images. It was from the early twentieth century, and was quite beautiful. She paused for a moment, then ran her finger down the page, counting. She whistled and shook her head. "I guess I never noticed how many fables there are with foxes in them."

As Florence began to shut down the room and prepare for bed, Rilke stood and stretched. He had liked Siena's story, and had been enjoying a new book until Fen had become upset. At that point he had stared at the page reading the same sentences over and over again. He was afraid that he would be pulled into the argument. It wasn't that he didn't have an opinion. But he sided with Fen.

The fox was right. The more Rilke read about history, the more conflict and violence he encountered. All life was ranked in a hierarchy that erased some individuals from it, or placed others at the bottom. Humans were always at the top and everything else below them. Trees, the Earth that sustained them, baby rabbits in their burrows and people like his ma, they all mattered less. In a different time, women like Siena and Florence would have been criminals. The rules, customs, and stories of the past didn't make sense. It was as if they were written for a world with only one unhappy person in it, not the world that actually existed and all of the beings that made it interesting and colorful. The more he learned, the more he questioned, and it seemed only the fox saw the world clearly.

Still, he knew that it was his task to help Fen understand that Florence had meant no harm. What's more, it was important for Fen to see the differences between human beings, because not everyone was kind. This was a point Brynja had been clear about, and he had begun to see evidence of this fact in everything he was reading.

"I'll talk to Fen," Rilke offered with a yawn. He gave Florence a quick side hug and waved good night to Siena who nodded back as she gathered the slumbering puppy into in her arms. Rilke jogged up the stairs, his flashlight on and his book under one arm.

"Fen?" Rilke shone the light around the room. He walked around in the dark for a moment then saw something flashing under the bed. It was the info pad.

Rilke knew the fox was reading data so he prepared for sleep. Once snuggled under the blankets, he sent out a thought to the fox who was nestled under the bed frame.

"Hey."

"Hey, yourself."

Rilke could sense how down she was. He imagined she was blue, perhaps a mournful cobalt.

"Try red. With a white tip on my bushy tail. To make it easier for the hounds to find me and rip me apart."

The image in Rilke's mind disturbed him, but he knew Fen felt much worse. He could hear the self-loathing, the disgust.

"Why don't you come up here, where it's warmer? I'll even give you half the blanket." He patted the comforter and waited.

"According to Aesop, 'The wicked deserve no aid.'" She offered Rilke a summary of the story she had just finished. A fox was caught in a trap and tried to persuade a rooster to help him. The rooster instead alerted the barnyard, the farmer arrived, and "that was the end of Mr. Fox."

Rilke remembered some of the things he had been

reading about that week. The new words he had learned and the pictures he had seen. But these were not what she needed to hear about at that moment.

"Fen, that was a long time ago. People don't do that any more. And Mr. Sangreave would never do that to you." Rilke thought it might help to reassure her that she was safe. But he didn't know how to explain why it had ever been like that in the first place.

Then he remembered the way he and his uncle would sometimes bait the alligators with wooden pegs and foul-smelling offal. Once the gator had taken the bait, they could pull the gator closer to the boat. The rest, though done as quickly as possible, seemed brutal to him now. He had not eaten the meat of an animal since the train ride from Savannah. He had not considered it until recently, thinking about hunting and the way he, as a human, had interacted with animals before he met Fen.

"Sangreave would think about killing me if I ate his chickens."

The youth cast about for a response, but found none.

She went on, quoting a passage from the same story: "'No doubt he was hungry, but that was not an excuse for stealing.'" There seemed to be more she wanted to say, but didn't. Rilke listened, and felt an indirect thought that Fen had left unattended.

"Canto didn't treat you as property, but a friend." Rilke waited, feeling almost like he was on the boat with his uncle, throwing out the line, both worried that there would be nothing and worried that there would be movement. The part he feared the most was not knowing the size of what they might bring alongside the boat. And now, it was impossible to know what Fen had been reading, and how much she was holding back.

"It's more than that." She sounded choked.

"Go ahead." But he wasn't prepared for the onslaught of examples.

"One 'hero' tied three hundred foxes together by their tails and sent them running through fields with torches behind them." Rilke found the image disturbing. Not only the image of the burning foxes, but also the fields on fire. It didn't seem heroic to him, but something else. A bit more like an apocalypse.

Fen offered another, then another, and yet another example . . . hounds baying and chasing after foxes for sport as people rode horses across countrysides in pursuit. Foxtail hats and coats. Taxidermy foxes positioned to look alive and snarling. Whole farms breeding them for their furs. "In some parts of the world foxes were seen as demons who tricked human men into loving them . . . Rilke, it's terrible!" She made a squealing whine that sounded fearful, and he wanted to comfort her, but he didn't know how. Instead he waited for the snuffling under the bed to cease.

"Did you read anything else about foxes?" he asked, hesitantly.

"Yeah," came the answer from under the bed.

"And?"

"They live on every continent except Antarctica. Only humans are more widespread."

"Imagine that. So we've been together a long time. Tell me more."

"A fox den or a group of foxes is called an 'earth,' like our planet." Fen was pleased with this. The Earth was larger and greater than everything. "But foxes are usually alone."

"What else did you learn?" He wished for something happy as he was growing warm and sleepy.

"My ancestors would have only lived for a couple of

years, maybe ten at most." Rilke held his breath. "But with my modified genetics and domestic lifestyle, I might live to fifteen or twenty."

"Would Canto add your memory pin to his next companion?" It was a difficult question to ask, but Rilke had begun to wonder about this more as he thought about Grif and Siena.

"I don't know." She sounded tired as well. It had been a stressful evening, and he knew that the coming days would be harder as they figured out how to manage the growing list of repairs needed on the farm. Maybe it would warm up soon. He was eager to help Siena and Florence get ready for spring.

It was quiet for a while and neither of them thought about anything beyond sleepy thoughts. Outside, the wind hurled ice crystals against the glass. In the quiet dark, it sounded like bells.

Fen dreamed far into the ancestral spaces where foxes had always lived, in the earth.

"Hello?"

In the dream, she walked a long hallway that seemed to have no end. Finally, she reached a cul-de-sac. As if from nowhere, a cat appeared and asked Fen what one should do when in danger. Fen was confused.

"Who are you? Where am I?" And to these questions the cat merely brushed against her, continuing toward a path which had just opened in the side of the burrow. It was a small door, shimmering a bit along the edges, but Fen followed, curious to see where the cat led. In the dream, she remembered the cat she had been, and felt its mind press against her memory. *Hide.* As she began to run to keep up with the bouncing tail of the cat, soon she realized she was chasing a phantom of what had been.

Fen continued along the path which was subtly illuminated by tiny glowing stones. Soon, she came to another dead end. As if from nowhere, a dog appeared and began to bark, asking her what she should do if threatened. Fen was frightened.

"I don't understand! What do you mean?" And to these questions, the dog lunged as if to bite her, and she ran down a dark tunnel that had just opened, with the snarling dog following fast behind. In the dream, she remembered the dog she had been, and felt its mind press against her memory. *Run.* As she felt the breath of the dog fast on her heels, she ran into a darkness with no direction, into an abyss where she began to fall uncontrollably. Now Fen was just trying to find the earth below her as the dog disappeared into the nothingness.

When she landed, it was in another burrow, soft and spacious. The scent of age and ruin was all around her, and it triggered another memory. The yacht. The air and the wind that night that was being pushed up from the tropics. And another memory, this one of fire.

The fire.

Fen remembered the way Menora's scarf had been flying in the sudden breeze, then Marion's drunken cackle as the twin sisters danced together on the deck. Misi and Beale were in a chair several meters away, she in his lap, their kissing mouths making noises that Fen could not ignore, though she tried. Menora and Marion spun into one another, singing out of tune to music that was far too loud, the scarf wrapping around them, then flying out like a pennant. The wind was picking up.

Then there was fire, the tilting deck, the continuous sounding of the bell and the ship's horn, the flare flying up into the sky as a magnificent fuchsia-colored arc of exploded light. Fen ran across the deck, and there was no time, no way to see where Canto was or how to find him. Misi and Beale were screaming and struggling with their life jackets as they ran toward the boats. And everywhere, the freakish wind that began to force the waves higher.

"What tricks do you have for survival, you naughty fox?" The voice shook down around her, as if it came from the walls of the burrow. Then there emerged from the darkness a shimmering being that absorbed the light around it, even as it seemed to reflect it all back. But it did so trickily, as if the forms the atoms took could be anything, and could assume any form. A tiny fox with red eyes took shape, silvery-black with white around the edges.

"I've been watching you. I think you know how bad you are." The fox grinned a little, showing a row of needled-teeth.

Fen shook her head and backed away. The fox continued.

"The fire was your fault. You wished it on everyone there! You know you did." The fox took one step toward Fen, who took another step back.

"I . . . I did nothing of the kind! Canto was on that boat! I never—"

"Ah, but you did! I saw you! Then you jumped into that lifeboat and left everyone to die. It's just what everyone expects of a fox like you, *bad thing*." The creature laughed, a screeching titter that hurt Fen's ears.

Fen took another step back as the shadowy fox stepped toward her again. His teeth were sharp, and flashed in the light. The red eyes pulsed with a greedy excitement.

"You think you care about Rilke, but he is human like the rest. They all hate you, because they know you will betray and kill them! You nasty vermin, I see your heart." The beast took one more step and opened its wicked, gloating smile, the kind that takes the heat out of any warm place.

"N-n-no . . . they are my friends! I would not hurt them." This last was a terrified whimper. She felt her tail press against the wall of the burrow that seemed ready to close around her and swallow her up. She panicked, as images of Canto on fire and drowning interspersed with other images, of Rilke, falling from a mountain's edge, led there by a fox in the mist, but then abandoned.

"Yes, you know it's true. You'll betray him! He's safer with you dead! Mark my words!" And then the monster leaped toward her, and she squirmed in terror against the burrow in a scream that came from everywhere at once.

"No! No! I will not! I'm a good fox!"

Fen was thrashing under the bed and screaming so loudly the whole house came running. Rilke was already there, trying to calm Fen down. Her eyes rolled around wildly as he tried to calm her. She did not see him, but instead, the monstrous fox.

"Ow!" Rilke jumped back and hit the wall near the window with his back, and then his head. A small picture frame crashed to the floor and Siena rushed in with a broom, her long hair flying about her face, barely awake.

"What's wrong? What's happening?"

"I don't know! Fen bit me!"

He'd no sooner said the words than Fen tumbled out from under the bed and went streaking through the house crying in her weird little way that only foxes know. Grif, ears standing straight up, decided this was a new game and took off after her.

Siena came over and shone a flashlight on Rilke's hand, which was bleeding. It wasn't too deep, but her teeth had punctured his skin.

"That's not like her. She didn't mean to. I think that she was in a nightmare." He held his hand, pressing it to slow the bleeding, and Siena looked worried in the dim light.

"Let's go clean you up."

Just then, Florence showed up at the door with a solar lamp in hand. "What's wrong? Fen just about ran over me, and Grif was tearing after her."

"Fen bit Rilke. She was dreaming and he was trying to wake her."

"Let's take a look. Siena, go find Fen and make sure she's okay. I'm sure Grif thinks she's playing."

Siena left and Florence patted Rilke on the shoulder. "I'm afraid some of the stories may have upset her. I feel bad now for ever letting her have the info pad."

Rilke understood why Florence felt bad but he also knew something else was wrong. When he was trying to wake Fen, he felt her terror, and it was a fear of something real, of some real threat, not a storybook farmer or a pack of hounds in a hunt. It was related to the yacht in some way, because he knew the feelings were ones she carried deep, the ones that threatened to break through whenever she tried to remember that night. Regardless, he worried that there were things he could not help Fen with, and whatever she was running away from was something only she knew the shape of.

The Meeting

"Letter for Rilke!" Siena said as she came in the door. Without the truck, they depended on Sangreave and his wife to bring the mail by. The mail ran more efficiently when folks went down to the station and picked it up themselves. Florence worked out that two jars of canned peaches was a fair price for Sangreave's trip from the post office to the end of the driveway. Apparently he agreed.

When Rilke studied the envelope, he first felt how heavy it was. The surface was not paper, but some other material, meant to be retained or recycled. There was always more information in a document like this than what could be conveyed on paper alone, Florence pointed out. Siena tried not to hover, but she was also curious about who had known to send a letter to Rilke here. Then she remembered the night Fen and Rilke had arrived. Someone had called Florence to make sure they were safe. Someone had also given Rilke a letter of identification and retrieval, for the end of the journey. So what was this?

"It's from Brynja." Rilke was excited and his eyes searched the room. "Fen?"

"I'm right here." The fox stood eagerly by, curious as well. She looked a little disheveled, but as the winter began to recede, she was looking more like a wild fox than ever before. She allowed her coat to appear natural, often the orange-red of the largest true fox. There was a bit of a molt beginning, which marked her with sporadic white patches. Someone might think she had mange, but it was just the seasonal loss that any natural-born fox was subject to. Still, she was no natural fox. She had also begun sleeping under Rilke's bed. Florence was lately finding food where the fox had hidden it for later. But Florence never brought it up. She just gathered up the spoiled food that was only half eaten, and tossed it in the compost.

"Open it! Let's see what it says," Florence said without shame. Her mind was already playing with fantastical possibilities.

Rilke hesitated, realizing that everyone had gathered around him. He liked the attention.

He cleared his throat. He was about to read it aloud, but froze with his mouth open. Then he closed it again in disbelief as he scanned the letter fully.

"What does it say?" Florence prodded.

"Brynja has arranged for me to attend school in Maine on scholarship."

"But . . ." Fen interjected weakly.

"She says she'll arrange for you to be returned to Canto." Rilke was studying the letter carefully, as if none of it was actually meant for him but someone else. He looked at Fen. "She uses different words, but that's what she means."

"And how did she say it?"

"It doesn't matter."

"But it does, Rilke." The fox turned away, no longer interested, and left the room. Siena and Florence remained quiet until Rilke let out a breath and sat down at the kitchen table. It was smaller than the dining room where they'd eaten their first meal together and it was near a window that looked out on the courtyard. Rilke sometimes liked to sit here and read while watching the birds outside. The snow had finally melted, but now the ground was soggy with rain.

"I think she means for me to travel north by rail, at her expense. She also said something about sponsoring any treatment I might need."

"What does she mean by that?" Florence sat down at the table and tried to choose her words carefully.

"When I was on the train, I passed out. We assumed I'd been drugged. That did happen, but it also turns out that I have a mild allergy to pecans."

Siena shifted her weight to the other foot and was equally cautious with her question. "How does Brynja know that?"

"I guess she took a sample of my DNA while I was passed out. She does this all the time." Rilke found that saying the truth aloud didn't make him feel better, but he feigned a lack of concern. He put his head in hands and laced his fingers under his curls, massaging his scalp. All of this was a bit too much.

"You mean she is a contractor. A recruiter." Siena didn't mean for her to throat to tighten when she said "recruiter," but the end result was a cough that helped her conceal her contempt. Florence looked around the room and then back at Rilke.

"There was more. About Fen?" She spoke softly, so the fox wouldn't hear.

Rilke nodded.

"Fen might not be exactly herself. Brynja had to remove a pin. She was able to have it repaired, but it's core data. She sent it to a vet in Atlanta, which is where I'd need to go to meet her, in two weeks." Rilke looked at both of them. Florence looked green. Siena looked overheated. He was sure he looked similarly off balance. "*If* I decide to do that."

Both women nodded and seemed to relax.

Siena put her arm around Florence and pulled her close. "You need to do what's best for you and Fen."

Rilke glanced at each of them and sighed. "That's not all."

"Oh?"

"She has information about my father. She knows who he is. She says she'll tell me in Atlanta."

"Should you choose to go." Siena added, still squeezing Florence.

"Right," Rilke said.

"What kind of school? The one she said she'd gotten you into?" Florence had remembered this was the greater decision, and everything else hinged upon it.

"She doesn't say."

"But she assumes you'll want to go. Did she say why she pulled so many strings?"

"I think it has something to do with my scan. But she also said that she looked at my information 'unofficially.' So this is not a recruitment, and I'm not in a contract. She just wants to help."

Florence and Siena both nodded, but Rilke sensed that it was the kind of nod people make when they really mean to say "bless your heart." Neither of them said another word, but kept nodding and smiling. Finally, Florence broke the spell with a clap of her hands.

"Who's hungry? And where's that pup of yours, Siena?

He chewed my new shoes last night." Florence went in search of Grif. Siena shifted around uncomfortably, trying to work up an excuse of her own.

"You take as much time as you need to think. I'm going to go call about that truck part again." She started off in the same direction as Florence, then turned toward the office, where the phone was. "In case I need to take you to Atlanta."

Rilke nodded morosely, and looked back at the letter in his hands.

Rilke had settled into the chair near the window at the desk and was looking out on a gray sky that promised rain. He hated these wet winter days that drug on at the end of spring and made it seem far off. He watched as the wind pushed the tree around for a minute, and its leafless branches with tiny tight buds tapped once or twice against the window pane. Then there was a knock at the door, which he'd been expecting.

It was Florence. She'd brought his laundry in and had set it on the floor beside the bed. She had been clear from the outset that she would not fold his laundry for him, and Rilke had never asked her to. But they did have a lesson one evening about how to tuck pieces of clothing into neat squares, packets that could condense his whole wardrobe into one drawer. He had taken to folding clothes immediately. He made it a kind of meditation, and Florence always brought his clothes up from the drying racks and left them in the basket as she did now.

Florence turned as if to leave, but Rilke knew this was a pretense. He made it easier for her by breaking the silence. "What do you think I should do?"

She stood there for a minute and then walked over and sat on the edge of the bed. She crossed her arms and regarded him. Rilke thought she looked this way whenever she wanted to understand something that troubled her.

"How do you feel about this woman?"

"Brynja?" Rilke knew where this was headed.

Florence looked expectant while trying not to pry. He could tell she just wanted to help. But he had known for a long time how he felt and it was easy to say it aloud because it was the uncomplicated truth.

"She's a nice person, but I think she's used to making decisions that affect other people and sometimes she has to make them whether or not she wants to."

Florence nodded. Then she put her thumb on her lip, proceeding even more carefully into discerning Brynja's influence. She wanted to be sure that Rilke was making the choices that were best for him and Fen.

"Sugarfoot—do you like her?" Then she raised her chin up in a smooth gesture that signaled emphasis, while Rilke worked to parse where the emphasis was supposed to land.

"Like her? You mean, do I want to kiss her?"

Florence leaned forward a bit, studying his face. Rilke looked down, shy and unsure, but thoughtful.

"Kissing isn't—I feel a kind of love, or at least what I think is love . . . for you, Siena, and Fen. Sometimes I think I loved my Uncle Afi. Maybe my ma."

"That is a kind of love, but there are other kinds of love. Me and Siena, for instance. When I met her, I couldn't speak I was so dumbfounded. She was so beautiful to me, all the words just went out of my head. You ever feel that way for someone?"

Rilke shook his head.

"Do you think you just haven't met that special person yet?"

Rilke shook his head again, still avoiding her gaze. "I've

never wanted . . . I don't know." Searching for feelings in himself that were like what Florence had described, he started to feel disappointed that he couldn't give her the answer she wanted. Unconsciously, his shoulders began to curl in and he studied his hands. "Maybe—there's something wrong—"

"Baby, no. That's perfectly alright. You have so much love in you." Florence smiled and touched his shoulder, and he slowly relaxed.

He looked up at her. "Is it okay if I never have those feelings for anyone?"

"I found what I needed with Siena, but maybe what you need is different. Maybe you just need to keep looking, and find what makes you happy. All the best relationships come from friendship." Florence watched as Rilke considered her words. The relief crept over his face slowly at first, but was thorough. At least he didn't have to think about it anymore for now.

She hugged him and they both sat for a minute without saying anything.

Once she was sure Rilke felt better, Florence returned to her original concern. "Do you trust Brynja? Can you be sure of her motivations?"

Rilke looked down at his shoe, and the spot where Fen usually slept, under the bed. He had to think, but it was hard when Florence was asking him so many questions about feelings that led to other thoughts, other emotions, ones that he had never completely found answers to.

Brynja had known so much about Fen's programming that it scared him. First there was knowledge that made a being like Fen possible. But that same knowledge also allowed people to made choices for her kind. Then there was the knowledge about him that she had gained somehow.

Maybe when he had passed out. Maybe when he threw up. In Brynja's world, Fen had no rights and in fact was property, just as he was a resource. A human resource, who could enter a contract voluntarily and accept benefits like special medical treatments. International law had pulled the world back from certain catastrophe when they established limits on genetic engineering and artificial intelligence. But it had taken too long to find that balance, and now that he knew more about history, he doubted that Brynja's motivations would ever be clear to him. She would be able to justify anything with her rhetorical training.

"Yes, I can trust her," and he knew it was a lie when he said it, but so did Florence. It was a fair enough compromise.

"So she wouldn't openly betray you but she'd have her own ideas about how you could be useful."

Rilke allowed a smile to dance on the corner of his mouth but nothing more. Florence was a complete pro, he decided, as his uncle sometimes said of people who had an uncanny ability to see through deception but also to convey it, or participate in a lie with no reaction.

"So the question is, how much of a help is she to you, in proportion to what you could lose if she played her game too freely." Florence said this to herself as much as she seemed to say it to Rilke. "She just likes knowing that you owe her a favor." Florence nodded again, answering her own questions. "Well, honey, you *will* make your own choices. And what about Fen?"

She said this last part without expecting an answer either, but Rilke felt the question to be unfair.

Fen thought so too, from the deepest, darkest place under the bed where she listened. She hadn't meant to eavesdrop, but she had begun to feel unwell again and it wasn't enough to park herself in the secluded nest that she normally occupied near the corner of the bed. She had craved unbroken dark, so she had continued to explore the under space of the bed, through comforters and rugs that no one seemed to remember being there.

As she had listened to the words spoken aloud she pressed further into the duplicitous, hidden minds of Florence and Rilke. She had heard the lies, and knew that love was at base of all of them. But it troubled her that she was becoming a wedge between Rilke's chances at a better life and a real family who could protect him. Already she saw it, the way his nose was always in a book these days, not just German poetry, but other works that were leading him onto new trails of wonder. She knew he wanted to see the world, but he was poor and without influence. He wasn't like Canto. Fen saw herself as a problem for Rilke now, and she felt her stomach tighten, along with her throat, as her eyes burned and she tunneled deeper into the blankets under the bed.

Fen waited until the house was asleep before slipping out the dog door and into the night of the courtyard. The puppy slumbered in his bed by the door through Fen's quiet escape, only rousing enough to make a small growl before nestling further down into the blankets. Fen had pulled one of the blankets over the tiny sleeping form and marveled over the little creature's perfect features. How complex life could be, she thought, suddenly aware that she could not remember when she herself had first acquired the memories of Mimi's past dogs and cats or if they had always been there.

She was no longer sure what it meant to be alive or to be a created thing. She only knew anything at all because of the brain she had and the one that had come to mean all of the added parts: the empathy pin, the memories, the added features that no natural fox had ever known. Somehow, this life, it meant moving forward and letting go. She was letting go of Rilke, Grif, Siena, and Florence. All of them had been kind to her, but she felt increasingly restless, and drawn by an insistent force that became stronger every day.

Was this also a feature of programming and artifice? She could not be sure. But she felt the drive to leave, and to walk, not necessarily to a specific place, but away. She would walk the Narrow Road alone, staying to the forest's line. And when she had to, she would ask a human for help. She wasn't afraid of discovery or even of being alone. She was only afraid of taking Rilke away from the closest family he had ever found. He could stay here and be happy with them. They could tend to the farm and he would learn from them what Fen could not teach.

Besides. What if the fox had told the truth? What if she had killed Canto, because she had hated Marion and Menora so much? Because she had wanted Misi and Beale to drown in their desire for each other. Or to burn. She didn't care.

There. She felt it. A kind of rage that only a bad fox would have. She could hurt Rilke with this anger. She had already bitten him, and even though she had cried to him in apology, and his hand had healed quickly, she had still done the worst thing she could have ever imagined. What if she did what she could not imagine, but was within her power to do?

Besides, Fen had her own future to attend to, and it was shaped by this self in her that wanted to be alone. She had seen enough to know that people were trapped in their own histories of staying and going. But she had been purposefully designed and she had every intention of fulfilling that purpose. She was to comfort Canto, to remind him of Mimi, even when Mimi was gone. Her purpose had always been to make him happy, and even this new companionship in Rilke had been a reminder only of Canto. So why was it so hard to jump up onto the box by the red flowers and out onto the shed's roof and over the fence?

Rilke didn't need her, came another thought. This one was faint, but derived from some part of her she could barely understand. It was like the feeling she had when Rilke had first picked up the pup and scratched behind its ears before cradling it in his arms. Though it was not something she had wanted, or could even enjoy (she could not remember ever being so small), the feeling still rattled around within her. There were other feelings too, like one that made her want to see if Rilke was sad when she was gone, or if he would even notice. Perhaps he would not care, and would be happy to know he had no hard decision to make. That she was no longer a burden to him.

There. That feeling was also one that came from a place that was not her programming, but adjacent to it. Or inside it. Or beyond it. She couldn't place it like a thing but she could say that it was indeed something she felt and could not deny, though there was no obvious cause for the thought or the feeling it was connected to.

Nevertheless, she hesitated on the edge of the roof as she eyed the top of the fence. There was no coming back after she made the jump. Once she committed, she would not return. And though the possibility of her leaving might be a part of her programming, just more evidence of her life as a machine, a created thing, she preferred to think that the spirit of her program, her purpose, was what made her want to survive and to believe that Canto waited for her somewhere. He was surely alive.

But maybe he was and he thought she was dead. Or, much worse, he might believe her to be alive but think she might be indifferent to him. For her, a binary was the sensible path, not a false dilemma by human standards. She knew the world was more complicated than zeroes and ones but then it all became a sense of scale, didn't it? And sometimes she could see the larger significance of things around her, and it was indeed, off and then on, positive and negative, but at velocities and at frequencies beyond her. It was or it was not.

She was to jump, or she would not. She could go back into the house, wrap herself around the puppy, and wait a bit longer for Rilke to decide. But he had delayed them, at first an entire winter, and now the early spring as well. She tried to think about what he feared, then she saw it was merely the leaving.

To go or to stay.

He did not need her. He was safer without her. She tensed her body for the jump she would have to make, almost at the end of her range.

She thought of the leaping foxes in the snow that Canto had often told her about. She smelled the snow on the air and realized she might see it again, even in April here, according to Siena and Florence. Then a new thought emerged, a fear for Canto, and a knowing of what she must do in order to keep him safe. That surety was all she had needed. Resolved, she leapt forward into the icy air.

And then she was the fox, and the night itself, which cloaked her. She befriended the night and the snow and the cold and her freedom in one fell swoop, and transformed into the shimmering darkness she had never felt so keenly till now. In that shade, she leaped like the ancestral fox had in the beginning of time. She felt the cold air waft up into her belly fur, and she felt the hard bite of the fence's edge against the soft pits of her forelegs and against her chest. Somehow she had just enough momentum to make it over and into the darkness alone.

The morning was gray and there was a dusting of snow on everything. But then the sun poked through and the whole house decided it was going to be a beautiful day. The ground was too warm for the powder, so it was gone by mid-morning. Everyone had a big breakfast, and at first, it just seemed that Fen was sleeping in. But there was something wrong. Even Siena felt it, and sometimes she could be a bit dense when noticing a change. But Grif kept trotting back and forth by the door to the courtyard, and whining in a way that revealed something was off.

"Have you seen Fen?" Florence was the first to ask the question, then everyone halted in their cleaning up and rinsing mugs or plates. Even the circling pup stopped his anxious pacing and everyone looked at each other. No one had seen her.

First, they checked in all of the low, dark spaces. Under the beds. In Florence's tower behind the dictionary table. The hallway that had recently been repaired and reopened after the fallen tree had been cut up. The garage. All of the rooms. Under the couch. Then the search began to feel ominous.

"I can't sense her. Anywhere." Rilke was breathless, having come back from pulling everything out from under his bed. He was holding a small bone by his pinched fingers at arm's length away from him. It stank, and since no one ate meat, it must have been something that Fen had found on one of their recent walks. Maybe three days ago, Rilke surmised as he lay it on a piece of newspaper and washed his hands.

"Shew, Lord! That stinks! Take that out to the compost bin right away." Florence chased him and the paper-wrapped bone out the door and it was then that they decided to check the courtyard. Grif charged outside and ran immediately to the edge of the small shed where Fen had made her escape.

There was a small tuft of hair caught on the roof edge, strangely translucent, like optic fiber or scales. Everyone knew then that Fen had run away, and this meant there was no time to waste. Rilke dashed for the gate and Grif was just ahead, waiting for Rilke to open it for him. Siena grabbed her gloves. Florence wrung her hands a bit and said she'd stay at the house, but that they should hurry. She'd wait by the phone.

Once freed, Grif, Rilke, and Siena fled through the gate toward the woods.

Rilke ran after Grif who was speeding into the woods following an invisible scent. Siena was running too, but the strained breathing of the woman kept growing fainter as Rilke raced on, pursuing Grif. Did the dog really know where he was headed? Or was he leading them on in a game that only he knew the rules to?

The woods were wet, and more than once, Rilke's shoe slipped in the mud and he almost went down. Grif turned toward a small, snow-dusted hill, and as much as Rilke wished it wasn't where they were headed, the truth was clear. Siena had already stopped to catch her breath and was holding her side. Rilke's side hurt too, but he took a second to breathe more deeply, apply pressure with his fist, and continue on, dreading what he might find at the top.

Though there had been buds on the trees farther down on the farm, at this elevation there were none. The bare trees were stripped of life, emptied by the long winter, and around him there were other signs of the ice storms that had blistered the landscape. The ground was still part ice and part thaw in places, and crystalline where the dirt broke apart from itself.

His feet found the ledges created by small roots. He would lunge forward, grab a young tree trunk, and pull himself up when his mud-caked shoes slid in the loose leaves. Fallen sticks and twigs were clumped around the deadfall of the maples, which made for slow progress up the hill. Branches had shattered under the twin forces of ice and brutal wind, and lay in long parallel lines stretching up the bank, lodged against other trees.

Grif continued his lunging run uphill, leaping forward then pulling himself up just as Rilke was doing with the trees. Clearly the pup was expending effort which made the likelihood of their finding Fen more possible and likely.

"How are you doing, little guy?" Rilke ruffled the pup's ears. Grif had stopped as well, panting.

There was blood on the leaves near him.

Rilke's heart skipped.

"Fen?" He didn't want to imagine the scene waiting for them once they topped the hill. Still, Rilke's mind was empty of other thoughts that might signal that Fen was nearby.

With a rush of renewed energy, Rilke scooped Grif into his arms and charged forward. Below, he could hear Siena's cursing as she too picked up the pace.

When Rilke crested the hill it was hard to say for sure what he was seeing.

Fen lay on her side and she was covered in blood. Beside her lay a mangled form that might have been a bird once, but wasn't any more.

Rilke quickly turned away and shielded the pup who struggled to escape his arms. But Rilke held on to him firmly and carried him to Siena who by this point was topping the incline and could see the bodies ahead. She glanced at Rilke with concern but took the wriggling pup from him. There was no need for Rilke to say anything aloud. She started toward the house with Grif in her arms, now beginning to whine and bark. He knew Fen was near but that nothing was right.

Rilke turned around and tried to focus his eyes, not on the blood, but on the form of the fox who was panting and sometimes shuddering with low choked sounds like sobs. Not like a fox at all, but more like a child.

Rilke stepped toward her and saw there was no visible injury, which meant the blood might not be hers.

"Are you hurt?"

The fox lay still, but faintly he heard a "no" come to him as if from the end of a long hallway.

"I'm going to take you home now."

He gathered her into his arms and she hung loosely, as if just a pelt, free of form or shape. He tenderly stroked her head and pressed her to his chest, trying to warm her. He could feel the small unprotected pads of her feet against his bare arm, and they felt ice cold, even though he had rushed out without a coat and was feeling the chill himself.

As he carefully made his way down the hill, he felt her limp body occasionally vibrate with grief. He saw brief flashes in his mind of the chickens, flying as she attacked each of them, wildly, without pausing between them. All dead, he sensed, or rather knew, from her memories.

"I couldn't stop," she offered weakly, "I was the fox they wanted."

Rilke continued picking his way down the hill, watching to see where Siena went with Grif so he could avoid encountering them on his way into the house.

"Who, Fen?" He didn't want to hear her answer as much as he needed to keep her talking. She was on the verge of entering some other world, teetering on the edge of what he was afraid to understand. But he had to know, especially if he was going to pull her back from her own destructive well of memory.

"The storytellers. They want a fox who raids farms and attacks birds . . . to justify killing them . . . the fathers who can't come home but lead the hunters away . . . the mothers with their kits, hidden in their earth, all destroyed . . . suffocated."

Again she fell apart in his arms and he squeezed her closer to him, certain now that the injuries were invisible, but all too real.

He had seen violence in his reading of history. The justified means to human ends, the choices to obliterate family groups and kinships, entire nations robbed of grandmothers and infants, sometimes in supposed retribution for some earlier crime, and in others, for much less, for a belief of moral superiority or social order. It wasn't right, and it made no sense.

How could humans kill innocents with such energy and intention unless there was some natural impulse in them toward murder that went beyond mere survival, was some other desire entirely? A selfishness, to keep the larger world for one's own kin? A vindictive lust to watch as others suffer? He thought of Samson's foxes, of the burning fields and the starvation that would certainly have followed such an event.

He thought of the death camps in the twentieth century, and the genocides of the twenty-first that went uncounted; the mass murders happening at the pace of first two, then three, then four a day until the structure of civil life fell away entirely. The genetic scans began as a way to isolate the violent strands and rout them out. And for the most part, they had been successful. But animals? Where were they in this project?

Rilke walked purposefully into the house where a worried Florence was already standing by. Grif had been sequestered in a side room where he barked and whined inconsolably. Florence waved Rilke toward the washroom that they had always used for Webb and sometimes for Siena when she'd been filthy with oil or dirt. The water was running softly and when Rilke checked the temperature, it was just a bit more than lukewarm. As he began to gently rinse the fox's coat, he gradually warmed the water which had turned red and then pink, until it was just plain water going down the drain and she could have been any thin, wet dog in the bathtub.

Except she was not a dog, and that part of it pained her, made her want death before she would see the ones she loved die because of her natural mind, the part that had been repressed in order to have this creature that could carry thought, but still had feelings of attachment and perhaps even love. It was a gift she had never asked for, this consciousness. And now with it, nature rebelled, the technology of two hundred years crushed by the code of not centuries, but millennia. She was a naked new thing, willing and wanting to die so that those she loved wouldn't have to.

"Stop, Fen, please stop." Rilke grabbed her chin and pulled her face up to his. "Look in my eye. You are unique. There is only one Fen. There will never be another Fen." Still ashamed and collapsing inward on her own misery, she looked up, shivering, but this time from cold.

"Wrap this blanket around her." Siena had brought an old wool throw, and Florence saw that it was Webb's blanket, the one Siena had wrapped him in when they were rushing him to the vet after the bear attack. It had long since been washed, but it still showed traces of the dog's blood in splotchy brown stains. It was the warmest, most precious blanket to her she could find, and Fen felt Siena's love for the old dog, and his for her.

Rilke immediately swaddled Fen in the blanket and

carried her to the couch closest to the cookstove. Here he sat with her and rocked, cradling her the way his mother had once when he was sick and she was sure he would die. The killing flu had been sweeping through the city, and most people stayed in if they could. He remembered it was the last time he had gone to school, because when the flu hit, the schools were closed for a long time after. His mother never allowed him to go back after he recovered. She said he was too weak. But he realized later she hadn't wanted him to be scanned, out of fear she would lose him forever. Maybe he could finally forgive her, he thought, because she had indeed loved him.

Fen's shivering began to ease just as the phone rang. Rilke continued to rock her and she drifted on his memories for a while and he on hers while Florence talked to Sangreave in the background.

Siena stood by the phone, whispering things for Florence to say or not say, and Florence spoke more loudly for everyone's benefit while pushing Siena out of the room.

"Yes, we're all fine here, you okay?" Florence glared at Siena who ran her hands through her long black hair and crossed her arms.

Florence glanced in at Fen, still on the couch.

"Is that so? Well, I'll be." The whole house listened as if one trembling ear.

"I'm sorry to hear that, Sangreave." Still she nodded and there were several punctuations of "my, my" and "oh goodness!"

"Rilke's still here. Oh yes, Fen is fine! She's just lying in here on the rug playing with Grif like a good little dog." Rilke hugged Fen to him, still rocking.

"Certainly, we'll make sure our birds are secure. No, we're good on meats, you know we're vegetarian, Sangreave.

Oh, really?"

Siena looked as if she were about to explode. Then she began pacing the room like she did when trying to figure out a problem.

"You were going to slaughter them anyway? Well, I'll be! But couldn't bring yourself to? Oh my!" Florence laughed nervously, but with a trace of relief. Siena came into the lodge partly to get away from Florence and the stress of the call, but also to check on Fen and Rilke.

"I'm going to bring Grif in so he can see you're okay."

Fen suddenly shivered, as if in a spasm of worry. Rilke reassured her that the pup hadn't seen anything. The puppy soon came bounding in the room with Siena jogging in behind him.

Grif was all over Fen, licking her and hopping up and down excitedly on his forepaws. She was overwhelmed by the dog's affection and made a soft chittering sound in return. Florence came into the room just then and plopped down on the couch, finally allowing herself to relax.

"What did he say?" Siena's worry had been that Sangreave might make the connection that Fen wasn't a dog. That had been Rilke's concern as well. Now he just felt bad about Sangreave's chickens and the inability to make amends without telling the truth about Fen.

"He said that he and the missus had been planning to host a chicken fry. Now they can. End of story."

Siena was flabbergasted. "It can't be that simple!"

"Sometimes you just don't know." Florence was mystified as well, and thinking back to the strange phone call. It wasn't unusual for Sangreave to host community get-togethers, but he normally didn't hesitate to slaughter his own chickens for the events. He must be getting sentimental in his old age.

"We still need to do something. But what?" Rilke knew that Fen felt worse than any of them, and he needed to find a way of assuaging her guilt to prevent her walking back down to Sangreave's farm dressed in tawny red fur with black ears. She had wanted him to be the farmer in the stories, to reinforce her own ideas about what she was, who she was, in the grand human narrative where she found herself.

"I was planning on going to the spring market with Sangreave. I'll just buy twice as many chickens and say I got them on sale." Everyone made agreeable sounds and only Fen remained quiet. She was grooming Grif lovingly with her teeth, and seemed calmer now. Her coat was still a pale version of herself, and she didn't try overly much for consistency. Her tail was two or three colors and her ears shifted from rust to sable as her ruff pulsed between silver, black, then pale gray.

No one said anything for a while, but sat in exhausted silence. There was a finality that had also settled on the room. It was spring, and there was nothing to do but walk. Even though Sangreave had not figured out Fen's true identity, it was only a matter of time. Rilke had already decided how he would reply to Brynja, and Fen rested her head on Grif while Rilke shared his plans with only her and no one else.

Siena and Rilke stopped in the street and she adjusted his tie. They had gone to a thrift store near the train depot in Gainesville and found matching maroon suits from the 2090s. It seemed the thing to do before a trip to the big city, and both were eager to show off their new style. Siena's hair was pulled back in a loose bun and a small earring glittered in one ear. Rilke's curly hair was wild as ever, waving up and around a face that appeared remarkably well-rested though they had stayed up late, talking and playing board games with Doll, Siena's friend from the depot. Even Fen was decked out with a shiny collar and leash, appearing to several people as some kind of spitz. Some thought her to be Finnish, Norwegian, or Belgian. But it was Brynja who called her disguise accurately.

Brynja was wearing a flowing white suit and her pale hair circled her crown and continued down her back in multiple braids. She seemed more relaxed than she had been on the train, and Rilke decided it must be the same thing Siena was struggling with, but in reverse. Siena was less comfortable in the city, and waved awkwardly across the atrium to Rilke and Fen as she found a seat at the bar. Soon she was talking with a fella next to her and Rilke knew that he and Fen would have all the time they needed.

"An Icelandic Sheepdog! Of course." Brynja clasped Rilke's hand in greeting and leaned forward to pet Fen. They had been to the vet that Brynja had paid to clean Fen's hardware and replace her temporary pin. There had been some happy moments when Fen was able to answer questions about Canto that she hadn't remembered before. She was also able to upgrade some of her drivers so that her camouflaging abilities were expanded. Best of all, Fen's molting was written out of her code which would have been a certain reveal of her species had it been allowed to progress unchecked. And finally, Fen could control her hormone levels in ways that could further conceal her. Being able to curl her tail at will made her even more convincing as a domestic dog. Fen was also pleased by the attention that people lavished on her as they admired her collar and shiny coat.

"We've been shopping," thought Fen toward Brynja.

"I can see that," Brynja said. Rilke was a sight to behold in his wide-collared vintage suit and sunglasses, which he reluctantly removed at Fen's urging.

"He's incorrigible," she said to Brynja. "Those glasses make him look ridiculous." Fen sneezed to underscore her point.

Brynja nodded toward Siena, who occasionally stole a glance toward Rilke and Fen. "I see you have a bodyguard."

"She insisted on coming. I couldn't stop her," Rilke looked down at Fen and squeezed her ears nervously. Fen lay down and put her nose in her paws like a good dog, even though she wanted to hop up in the seat beside them and order some fried tofu. Brynja had chosen an upscale restaurant serving Korean food, but they stayed in the exterior seating area that connected several tall office buildings together. It was more casual and allowed dogs, so long as they were well-behaved like Fen.

Rilke enjoyed seeing the city because it reminded him of Savannah, though he had only ever seen the new city's skyline from a distance. Now he was seated at a table inside a glass tower having sweet fizzy water in a crystal flute. It was beyond what he could ever have imagined.

Fen heard his thoughts and said "Oh no, it gets better," which made Rilke anticipate their journey even more. He was long past the resentment he used to feel when Fen compared everything against her own privileged world. Now he was eager to see it for himself and have the superlative confidence that was necessary for one to say things like, "No, my dear, the best curry is in Edmonton," or "Let us go see this gallery which cannot be nearly as fine as those in Toronto."

They ordered, and Brynja moved to the subject of their meeting. "Have you decided?"

Rilke nodded and sipped his second bubbly drink with endless refills. "Fen and I are going to walk."

Brynja accepted this coolly, as if she had already known what his answer would be. "But you're considering the school?"

"What kind of school is it?" He had already discussed with Siena the possibility that it could be a trade school sponsored by Brynja's human resource agency, or perhaps a military school.

"Liberal arts. You can study literature if you want. Or German poetry. Philosophy. History. Whatever you like."

Rilke seemed pleased, and a poorly-concealed smile danced in the corners of his mouth. "And we can wait until next spring if we have to?"

Brynja looked away and appeared uncertain. "We'll see. But you'll need to reach Maine before the weather turns. Your authorization expires then as well." She referred to the earlier paperwork she had prepared that would offer him support and processing free of interference, but within a restricted time frame.

"I want to take Fen to Canto myself." Rilke was direct, and there was not going to be a negotiation. Brynja liked seeing this change. Maybe they would make the trip just fine.

"You're lucky to have him watching out for you," Brynja said to Fen.

"She's my best friend." He looked down at the foxy dog who looked up at him expectantly, tongue lolling. "Even if she is a silly glutton for attention."

"So you're not accepting the editing treatment either?" This did surprise Brynja a little, considering that allergies were one of the more basic edits that everyone tended to want, especially since these changes didn't typically result in sterility. Most young people chose their own well-being over future progeny anyway.

"Not right now. Maybe when I get to Maine."

Their food arrived and the talk turned to lighter subjects such as the farm and how long Brynja would be in the city before heading out again, but further south and west this time. Rilke slipped Fen pieces of his fried tofu under the table and dished out some rice for her as well. She was pleased with this and Siena looked happy with her third lemonade, or what appeared to be lemonade from afar. Later she would tell Rilke it was "lemonade for grown ups," which seemed to amuse Fen for some reason.

The bill came and Brynja covered everything, even Siena's drinks, which pleased the woman immensely. Apparently they had been costly. The three of them would be taking the train back to Gainesville and staying with Doll tonight, Siena said, in-between hiccups. It had been kind of Brynja, yes indeed, and "very good to meet you," the same, and they had shook hands.

All four of them were saying their farewells and Rilke was confirming that he would let Brynja know where he was every hundred miles or so. Brynja expressed doubt that he would, and Fen said she would hold him to it. Just before Siena, Fen, and Rilke began to walk out the door, Brynja called Rilke back over to her for a moment. Fen stayed with the more-than-slightly-intoxicated Siena, who thought it hilarious that she was holding the leash, of two, maybe three separate Fens who all looked remarkably like little red dogs.

"What about your father? Did you not want to know?"

"No, I think it can wait." Rilke put his hands in his pockets and stood straighter. He liked being able to choose things for himself. Besides, it was never anything he had really wondered about, though others had always made it seem important.

"You mean it?" She was surprised, and he liked seeing her off guard for once.

"I never asked to be scanned, Brynja."

Brynja looked out the window at the pedestrian corridor

of the city center. A second later, the monorail glided silently into the largest part of the atrium further down into the plaza. Sparrows flitted among the rafters, either finding nests or trying for freedom, it was impossible to tell.

"I wanted to make sure that you wouldn't encounter any problems. People may ask."

Rilke looked at her long and hard, and for once, he seemed older than his age and it was a convincing maturity. Something had aged him.

"Knowing who my father is doesn't concern me right now. I'm sure he was a good man and had his reasons for staying away." Rilke did feel this to be true, and saying it aloud made something settle in him that had been restless during brief moments in his life. It had mattered sometimes, when he had been angry at his ma. When he had walked the stadium after she forbade him from going back to school, looking for something, anything to read. Something to take him away from his life the way a father might have. But he didn't feel this anger anymore and he was at peace with memories of Afi, who had been enough of a father for him in the times he needed.

"With your aptitude, you can do anything you want. But you're also going to need an identity that can be verified before they'll let you take Fen into Canada. I don't care whose fox she claims to be."

Rilke shifted his weight to his other foot and glanced at Fen who seemed to be either laughing at or laughing with Siena. The two of them were drawing the attention of security, and Rilke knew he was running out of time.

Brynja grabbed his arm gently. "Look, don't get sidetracked. Don't sign anything. For God's sake, don't let anyone scan you or open a contract. Call me first, and I'll be there as quickly as I can. You wouldn't make it a week in the ship lanes. Those are for a certain kind of guy—" she shook his shoulder a bit, "—which you absolutely are not. You're smart, sweet, kind. You don't need editing, okay? Just . . . stay away from pecans."

She smiled and he hugged her, which she appeared to tolerate, though it moved her nonetheless. She pushed a stray tear off her cheek and was stony-faced once more.

"You better get them out of here," she said, looking toward Siena and Fen. The two were being encouraged to leave the arcade by two frowning men in uniform. Both the fox and Siena were in hysterics about something, probably inappropriate, but amusing to them.

Rilke sent a final wave back to Brynja, who returned the gesture as she held her other hand near her cheek, calling a car.

The sun was bright as they left the gleaming mall. They had a train to catch, but the three of them took their time. There were still a few days left to enjoy each other's company and say goodbye. Florence would fret over them the last two days and cry most on the last. There would be dried fruit and savory protein sticks, some rice balls set aside for Fen. And a little over two thousand miles to go before they would see anyone they knew again, though anything could happen along the way.

Fen had the sensation of falling again, just like she had before, even though twice already she had startled awake on the corner of Rilke's bed. She had lain there bristling with excitement long after Rilke had fallen asleep, and now she was beginning to slip into that other world, the madcap realm of dream.

She found herself in a corridor, much like one she recalled from before. This time there was no cat, no dog, no fox, but instead a long straight path that seemed endless. Once or twice she had jerked awake, only to fall back into walking. She was beginning to wonder if she should turn around and go back when a voice spoke to her from just ahead. A pearl floated in the distance like a perfect, tiny moon, and the fox walked toward the orb with both curiosity and intention. Surely that is where the voice had come from. It had called her by name.

The fox felt no threat, even when the path narrowed and opened into a dark, blue sky, blackening as before a storm. Then, a glowing figure revealed itself to be a large luminescent fox, a ghostly trace of tails waving around her, much like sea grass along the shore when it is carried up by the swell and then let go.

She was beautiful, with pert triangular ears. She was smiling as if she had a secret, and then she walked up to Fen and sat before her, eye to eye. Fen sat down as well.

"Little fox, you have done well," said the shimmering, opalescent form.

Fen shifted to a pale lavender, and folded forward in deference. "But I'm afraid I have been bad, and in my anger, brought down a fire and a storm on a ship with many people on board." Fen thought a moment, then added, "There were also several chickens who died in my desire to destroy myself. I don't know what came over me."

The figure chittered at Fen and tilted its head.

"My dear Fen, you did not cause the fire or the storm. And the chickens . . . they paid the price of your believing what others said about you. It was the influence of the bad one, no more."

Fen considered this, and somehow, her memory called up another, this one buried deep, suppressed. It was of the fire's origin. There had been a pop, then a steady stream of smoke from an electric panel. Fen had smelled it and rushed to tell Canto. He had sent up the alarm, had placed her in the boat and had bidden her wait for him while he went to find others.

The wind and waves had become stronger, and she had hidden beneath the seat. There had been a thump, something had fallen, and the lifeboat had been released with only her in it. And that was the extent of the memory, but this one much clearer than before, much truer. She did not know what had happened to Canto after that, but only that she hadn't been the cause of the fire or the storm.

"Now, you must take care of this boy. He is lost, much like you are, and about to leave the only security he has ever known. But you need him, and he needs you."

Fen knew the fox was right, and didn't argue. She bowed and it was in her bowing that she fell headfirst into a dreamless sleep, the most restful sleep she'd enjoyed in several months.

When she did finally wake, it was just before dawn, so she slipped out of bed, stretching her body and tail in delight. She trotted through the hallway and into the kitchen, and hopped through the dog door into the courtyard. She jumped up to the small roof that she had leaped from just three weeks before. She was in a different place now, much relieved of the burden of guilt she had been carrying with her as if a heavy stone.

Briefly, she wondered if the right thing was still to leave with Rilke, but the answer was clear. He wanted to walk. He had made his choice. She could probably travel faster alone, but a voice inside her offered a warning.

Not yet, little fox.

Maybe the voice was the being from her dream. Maybe it was her own self, the best one, or perhaps it was Siena, still echoing in her conscience from months before. No matter. Whatever the source, it spoke the truth, and that was good enough.

Satisfied, she jumped softly to the ground and loped back inside to prepare for the trip. It was a great day for walking, and she was ready to begin.

Acknowledgments

Many thanks go to Catie, my first reader. Also to Macy Woods, Penelope Christian, and Kelsey Trom, who believed in this story and made it better. Much love to my family who have always been supportive of my pursuits. So many wonderful friends and colleagues, as well as students, who inspire me every day. Thank you also to SaveAFox Rescue, for their mission "To rescue and provide forever homes for captive-born, non-releasable wildlife." Much of the research I did about foxes involved watching videos that SaveAFox founder Mikayla Raines produces and shares with fans of the foxes they care for. Although the idea of a pet fox might seem appealing to many people at first, the reality is far more challenging. If you care about foxes and want to help, please check out saveafox.org and the good work they are doing.

About the Author

Living and working in northwestern Ohio, but originally from southern Appalachia, Liese Jeyd Hartman is an editor, writer, and professor of English. Liese longs for the forests and mountains of home and draws inspiration from the trail she loves. *Beyond These Winters* is Hartman's first work of fiction, and she hopes to continue Fen and Rilke's stories in more books to come.